AWAKENED DREAMS

Copyright © Annette Johnson, 2008. All rights reserved. No part of this book may be reproduced or transmitted in any form or by any means, electronic or mechanical, including photocopying, recording, or by any information storage and retrieval system, without permission in writing from the publisher.

Bedside Books
An imprint of American Book Publishing
5442 So. 900 East, #146
Salt Lake City, UT 84117-7204
www.american-book.com
Printed in the United States of America on acid-free paper.

Awakened Dreams

Designed by Morgan McConnell, design@american-book.com

Publisher's Note: This is a work of fiction. Names, characters, places, and incidents either are the product of the author's imagination, or are used fictitiously, and any resemblance to actual persons, living or dead, events, or locales is entirely coincidental.

ISBN-13: 978-1-58982-434-8
ISBN-10: 1-58982-434-2

Johnson, Annette, Awakened Dreams

Special Sales

These books are available at special discounts for bulk purchases. Special editions, including personalized covers, excerpts of existing books, and corporate imprints, can be created in large quantities for special needs. For more information e-mail info@american-book.com.

AWAKENED DREAMS

ANNETTE JOHNSON

DEDICATION

This book is dedicated to my entire family, with special dedication to Bill and Opal Johnson, Joyce and Charles Collier, my husband's parents, and my parents.

SCREAMING

Sara was awakened by screams. Screams of apparent and severe torture. They were agonizing. It was a woman, and it sounded as if her limbs were being torn off and her insides ripped out. It could have been happening in the next room; the screams were loud but muffled at the same time, as if someone were trying to quiet down the victim by putting a pillow over her face or a cloth gag over her mouth.

Sara was terrified. All she could picture in her mind was a bloodied woman, hands bound, mouth gagged, with a look of terror on her face, the last face she will ever make, frozen like a picture in time. The thoughts raced through Sara's mind as she listened. Her thoughts felt cloudy and unclear, but very real.

She jumped up into a sitting position. Dazed, she kept looking around, wondering if she was really hearing what she thought, trying to awaken herself and her senses without panicking.

"What the hell is going on?" was all she could say to herself in a low whisper, as if she was talking to someone in the room with her. Still very confused, she was wandering around in a foggy dream. Did she leave the TV on? She couldn't remember. Was she listening to some horror movie in which women didn't stop screaming? Why couldn't she wake up?

The horrible screams were echoing throughout Sara's apartment, bouncing off one wall and racing to the other side of the room. Sara tried to open her eyes to focus while stumbling out of bed, trying hard not to fall flat on her face. Her only thought was of the screaming woman. She felt such an urgency to find her and ease her pain.

It was like waking up in the middle of a nightmare, and now Sara was a part of it. Her mind still cloudy with sleep, Sara felt like she couldn't trust what her mind was telling her since she had been so wrong about so many things the past six months. Events lately were big blurs, she was having a hard time remembering anything, and she lost blocks of time as well. She wasn't sure what was real and what was just a part of her imagination. Was all of this a cruel joke her mind was playing on her? Like so many times in the past, she just didn't know.

There was a sudden loud burst of high-pitched screams. The noise seemed to go through Sara. She could feel it vibrate through to her bones. She kept asking herself if this was real as she tried to figure out where the screaming was coming from. She wasn't sure what room to look in first. The one thing that Sara knew was that, in the last six months, everything had changed. Nothing was for certain, not anymore.

A state of absolute necessity and panic began to take over. Sara needed to find who was screaming and make it stop. Otherwise, she would lose her mind. A panic swept over her that was so intense, she could feel her heart pounding right through her nightgown. With every scream worse than the last, she was becoming really frightened of what was happening and what she might find. Sara began to venture out of her bedroom, walking slowly at first and looking all around her to try and catch where the screams were coming from and follow its path. She tried to remain calm, stopping occasionally and pausing, walking as light-footed as she could so she didn't alert the woman's attacker that she was there. Sara didn't want to be next.

She could hear the floorboards squeaking with every step she took. She began to walk tip-toed, trying to remember which floorboards made the most sound and stepping around them. She swore she could hear her heart beating in her ears as if her heart was in her throat. Her breathing was erratic, and sweat was causing her long hair to stick to her face; Sara always sweated profusely when she was nervous or anxious.

Sara just stood there, trying to locate the direction of the noise, wanting to stop the screaming, needing to help the screamer. She realized the sounds were coming from outside her apartment, so she headed for the front door. Maybe it's coming from the hall, she thought to herself. She knew halls always seemed to echo even the slightest of sounds; it was always so eerie to her. Sara was very scared, but she was more scared of what she might find. She wasn't sure if she could handle finding a dismembered bloody body. She'd had enough of those kinds of scenes in the last several months. The sight of blood made her feel sick. Whenever she had blood drawn, she passed out.

Sara felt like she was walking a tight rope, rocking back and forth with her arms straight out, balancing between sanity and insanity and afraid of which side of that fence she might land on. This was one reason she hated living alone. She wanted to share moments of insanity with someone. Loneliness was hard on the mind, heart, and soul.

She wasn't sure what she would do if she found someone really being murdered. The way she was feeling, she would most certainly just freak out and run, hoping the person doing the crime would stop once he or she was found out. Hoping she might save a life or at least preserve her own. She couldn't let the screaming go on, not without finding out where it was coming from. She was so anxious that she placed her hands over her ears. All she wanted to do was scream, to drown out the screaming she was hearing with her own screams of insanity. That same tight rope kept popping up in her mind. North or South, Sara, which side was it going to be?

She kept thinking this was the normal fight or flight response to run and hide like a little schoolgirl. But deep down, she knew she was tougher than that. She had to be. She tried to thrive on being an independent woman who could handle anything and enjoy living by herself, but she knew she was lonely and wanted a more intense type of human contact. A boyfriend would have been real nice right about now. She began to whisper to herself, if I had a boyfriend here with me, he could be doing what I am doing right at this moment. She ended her statement with a little giggle and a smile on her face that faded with the next scream.

"What the hell am I thinking about?" she admonished herself more loudly. "What are you going to do when and if you find someone being hurt—scream at them, and tell them to stop? You're going to get yourself killed, that's what's going happen."

Sara opened her bedroom door, raced around her couch and past her fireplace. She opened the front door of her apartment so fast, it almost hit her in the face. The doorknob hit the wall so hard, it left a circular imprint. She jumped backwards out of the way, protecting her face with her hands. She slowly poked her head out the doorway and looked around in the hall. Nothing, only the sound of screaming. She pulled her head back into her apartment and rested it against the wall next to the door, closing her eyes, wishing the screaming would stop. Sara poked her head out her door again. The hall looked so long with its gray carpeting and dim lighting, the light casting an eerie shadow on the walls. Sara remembered seeing these kinds of shadows in several movies. The old haunted houses always seemed to have that staircase and shadows of someone creeping up them, wanting to kill someone or waiting to be killed themselves. Sara hated horror movies. She always wanted to tell those stupid girls not to go up there or in there or down there. They never seemed to listen to the screaming audience.

Sara's apartment building was equipped with an intercom system, a security feature she liked about the place. She felt safe here, knowing she knew who was at her door before she let them in. The second two-bedroom apartment was across the small hall from Sara's apartment and directly below that was Tom's apartment. Sara pressed the button that let her talk to anyone who might be standing outside.

"HELLO, HELLO, IS ANYONE THERE?" No response.

She ran down the hall steps, almost falling over her long nightgown as it dragged along the carpeted steps, catching the heels of her feet. Sara grabbed onto the railing to keep herself from falling head first down the stairs. By the time she reached the bottom step, her hand hurt from the friction of the wood against her dry skin and tense grip. Sara opened the outside entrance door, and the cool breeze sent a chill through her. She could feel the goose bumps rising and her hair on the back of her neck standing straight up.

Suddenly the sounds of pain and agony became less intense and more muffled. The screams sounded like they were echoing from the direction of the basement door located directly under the hall stairs. She slowly walked toward the door that led to the basement. Sara felt a little confused. In her apartment, the screams sounded like they were coming from the next room in stereo. But outside her apartment, they didn't sound as intense. Could the vents have made the screams sound so close?

The closer she got to the basement door, the more anxious she felt. She slowly opened the door and was hit by a wall of screams. She knew this was where the torture was occurring. Taking in a deep breath to gain some composure, she decided she needed to go downstairs; she needed to stop whatever was going on. She grabbed a flashlight from a small ledge at the top of the basement stairs and proceeded down, aiming a beam of light around and toward each step. When she got halfway down the steps, the screaming stopped. Sara looked around, disoriented, as if she was dreaming or maybe sleep-walking, and someone had just woken her up with a splash of cold water. She heard a loud bang, sudden and with fury. She turned and noticed the small amount of light that seemed to be behind her was gone. The basement door had slammed shut.

As Sara stood there, confused and unsure about what was truly happening here, she saw a light coming from the top of the stairs. A sliver at first and then it grew until the entire staircase was engulfed in a dim light. She didn't hear the basement door opening; her ears were ringing with the sounds of torture. That much she knew was true. That was about the only thing she knew was true.

"Sara!" Tom yelled. "Are you down there?"

Sara jumped and quickly turned around, almost falling down the stairs for a third time. She sure wasn't expecting to have anyone speak to her. It took her a moment to realize it was Tom calling for her.

"Tom, thank goodness it's you!" Sara yelled. Holding her chest she thought her heart would come out of her nightgown, now damp with sweat. It made her feel like everyone in the world could see through the thin white linen. She didn't care; she actually found it somewhat erotic, Tom being able to see through her nightgown. He had a little smile on his face which she would deal with later. Right now she had more pressing issues to deal with.

"Tom," Sara asked, "did you hear someone screaming?"

Tom looked at her, puzzled. "No, I came down here because I heard some stomping on the staircase like an elephant was running down the front stairs. Then it sounded like someone might have fallen. I also heard the basement door slam shut. I sure didn't hear anyone screaming."

"So now I'm an elephant," she said with sarcasm in her voice. She knew he was only joking, but she knew it might ease her mind a little if she could break the tension for herself. It might get her mind off the screaming she knew she heard.

Tom was walking down the stairs to meet Sara. He was tall and good-looking. He owned his own construction company, and it showed in his very muscular body. His dark wavy hair and big dark eyes gave him a Mediterranean look. Tom and Sara were now standing at the bottom of the basement stairs. She was thinking how much she loved this man; she could feel it in every inch of her body.

"The screaming stopped," she said. "Just stopped. I don't know what to think of it. I don't understand how I could have heard it in my apartment and you didn't."

"I don't understand it either," Tom replied, "but I swear I didn't hear any screaming or yelling or anything. I just heard you apparently running down the steps and then the basement door slammed shut. I really didn't know what was going on. I didn't know if someone was in trouble or not, that's why I came down here to investigate."

Sara thought maybe somebody was playing a radio too loud, or maybe the screaming she heard was from someone's TV or some hard rock song the local teens were listening to. But Sara didn't think so; she really thought someone was being murdered. No one could make those kinds of sounds unless he or she was being tortured to death, and she knew it.

Tom was looking at Sara oddly as she was trying to concentrate on what had just occurred. Sara didn't know if he was looking at her because of what she was wearing or just because he thought she was crazy. Seeing him standing there reminded her of her schoolgirl days. She blushed and felt a burning sensation run through her. Her body let her know it was still alive. She felt a need she had almost forgot about, the need to be with a man. A moment of false comfort and quietness seemed to fill the room.

"Well, the only other explanation was that maybe a bunch of kids were down here, and they heard me coming so they ran." Sara didn't sound convincing to Tom or even to herself.

She thought she sounded like a child who had just been caught trying to take cookies from the cookie jar and now had to sound as innocent as she could to avoid punishment.

Tom asked Sara, "What were you going to do if you did find someone being hurt down here?"

"I don't know—hit him where it hurts with my flashlight, I guess," Sara shrugged as she raised the flashlight in a stabbing motion to show Tom what part of the anatomy she was talking about. Tom placed his hands over his groin and grimaced—he got the picture. "Maybe if he thought someone was down here, he would have stopped," Sara continued.

"Sara, you could have been hurt if an intruder was down here," Tom said with his hand on his hip in an authoritative gesture. "Did you want to be the next victim if a burglary was going on down here? Or a party by a bunch of kids on drugs? You know they don't realize what they're doing on that stuff."

"I can take care of myself, you know." Anger now filled the room in the tone of her voice and the echoes throughout the room. Sara was mad. Tom was treating her as if she was incapable of taking care of herself, something she had been doing very well for many years.

Sara looked at Tom and replied in an annoyed and sarcastic voice, "I don't care what you think. I was going to try my best to stop whoever it was. I was going to do whatever I could. That's the problem with people; they don't want to get involved with anything or anyone anymore. People don't give a crap. What if I could have stopped a person from getting killed or prevented someone from getting raped? That kind of crap isn't going to happen if I can help it, regardless of what might happen to me!"

Tom just stood there looking at her. He was very impressed with her independence and assertiveness, and at the same time, he was furious with her. He was very attracted to Sara and didn't want to see anything happen to her. He wanted to protect her, keep her safe. He wanted her in his arms, to feel her next to him, to kiss her. He wanted to be closer to her than he was.

The way he was looking and smiling at her made Sara feel as if he was flirting with her, and she felt relieved. This was the first time in a while that she felt any kind of closeness with Tom. She felt like a schoolgirl again. She could feel her cheeks becoming flushed and was thankful for the dimly lit room.

Tom and Sara spent thirty minutes searching through the entire basement, finding nothing. "Well, no bogey men down here tonight," said Tom. "Now I have to get up early in the morning to catch a flight to Chicago on a business trip, so I guess I'll say good night. Do you want to call the police, maybe make out a report or something?"

Sara said, "No, I think I'll just go back to my apartment. I'll see you in the morning or whenever you get back from your trip. Why are you going anyway?"

"Just meeting with some potential clients," Tom replied. "If it pans out, it will make a big difference in my business. Listen, please, if you hear anything else, don't come down here by yourself. Come and get me first, OK? I really don't want anything bad to happen to you." Tom stood there with his finger pointed at her. Sara stared at his finger as if she was looking down the barrel of a gun. All she wanted to do was to bite it off.

She said in a condescending manner, "I hear you. OK, I will."

"Sara, I'm not trying to be a dad here," Tom said gently. "I would just prefer if you come and get me. You just never know what could be down here, and I don't want you to get hurt, that's all."

"OK," Sara said. "I promise, I will."

Tom could see that she meant it and was relieved as he led her up the stairs and into the apartment building hallway. Sara went back to her apartment and Tom did the same.

Something wasn't sitting well with Sara. She felt Tom's trip was more than he was saying, and that made her very nervous. She didn't need him poking around in her business where he didn't belong. But she had another problem. She had gotten to know him well in the last six months of their on-again, off-again kind of relationship, and she loved him, even if he annoyed her. She had never had such deep feelings for anyone before. It was as if he touched her soul somehow. But she knew it wouldn't last. Things just didn't work out for her in the romance department.

TOM AT HER FRONT DOOR.

When Sara got back into bed, she drifted off to sleep almost instantly. Several hours later, suddenly Sara was awakened from her deep sleep, this time by someone knocking hard at her front door. Whoever it was trying to turn the doorknob, trying to gain entrance. She thought it might be the same person who was hurting the person downstairs earlier. Maybe she had interrupted whatever it was they were doing and now was coming for her.

Sara heard the front door finally give way and crash to the floor. The intruder was inside her apartment. Sara froze in her bed as if she were a statue, afraid any type of movement would make the situation worse. The adrenaline flowed through her veins, and her heart began to pound as the sweat began to pour. Then she saw the shadow of a person, and she held her breath. Not the dim light casting shadows on her walls like so many times before, but a true shadow moving slowly across the room. She could hear footsteps coming closer and closer as the floorboards creaked under the weight of the intruder. As the intruder came closer, her heart pounded louder and faster, and her breathing became quicker and heavier. She was unsure of what to do; the phone was in the kitchen. She began to panic…a very large person entered Sara's bedroom. There wasn't enough light in her bedroom to see him. She could only see the shadow of darkness that encircled the intruder's face. Sara could only stare in horror as the intruder took another step toward her.

When the light fell across his face, Sara immediately recognized Tom. "What the hell are you doing here?" she yelled in both fear and relief. "You scared the crap out of me! And why the hell did you break my door?"

Tom didn't say a word. He just stood there, his black eyes staring at her, blank and unseeing, and she was becoming very scared. This wasn't the Tom she loved. It was a scary clone of him that looked like he wanted and could cause some serious damage. She could see his lips moving, but nothing came out. No sound and no voice, just movement. She remembered this look; she had seen it many times before with her mother. It was the look of a completely insane person. A person who had his own party going on inside his brain, his own reasons for doing things. A remorseless person with violence in his blood, flowing through him like a bad virus.

Sara repeated herself, only this time her voice convulsed with rage. "What are you doing in here? Why did you break in to my apartment?"

Nothing still. Sara knew this wasn't the man she fell in love with. Where was that man?

Tom was holding something in his hand. It was an axe. Sara screamed in horror, covering her mouth with her hands to muffle the sounds that were escaping her. Sara's thoughts turned into complete terror when she realized Tom was out to hurt her…no…no! He meant to kill her, but why?

Sara never felt so scared in her life. Her heart was pounding so fast, she couldn't catch her breath. Sweat was running down her neck, and her hands were shaking. Sara remembered this feeling; her mom had caused it many times in her life. She slowly began to remove the covers, trying not to alert Tom to her actions, while looking around for something to defend herself with. Sara wasn't sure how far she could go before Tom jumped on her and began hacking her to pieces. She needed to be as cautious as possible. She needed to get out of there, but she didn't want to make any fast moves.

Just then, Tom took a step closer to her and switched the axe from his left hand to his right. He began to twirl the handle of the axe, and she could hear it making a whistling sound in the air. Sara knew he was teasing her, and that this axe was meant for her and only her. Her heart was still pounding fast, and she needed to get a handle on it before she passed out and sealed her fate. Deep breaths, she reminded herself. Sara she knew her life would end soon, but not without a fight. If

Tom was going to hurt or even kill her, she was going to defend herself, and maybe do a little damage of her own.

The corner of Tom's mouth turned into a small grin. His teeth looked different, like sharp, black needles that could bite her and rip her skin to shreds. She could feel the fear in the pit of her stomach. A wave of nausea came over her, and her hands began to shake again. This man had gone crazy: Tom had gone crazy. When Tom smiled at her, just one corner of his lip turned up in the most eerie way; he looked almost animalistic with those black eyes and blank stare.

The only way out was to try to run over the bed. As she tried, she became tangled in her sheets and blankets, falling backwards, striking the back of her head on the corner of the nightstand. Sara could feel the burning and pain that seared through her head. She did not lose consciousness, but her head was spinning, and she could feel the room going darker and darker. Her voice was becoming more distant as she kept trying to tell herself to stay awake. Sara knew if she passed out, she would become Tom's victim, hacked into pieces.

Tom walked over to her slowly, stalking her in the moonlight. She could sense he knew she was hurt; the copper smell in the air told him she was bleeding. He didn't act like someone who was in a hurry to kill. Sara got the impression he knew he could take his time, play with her a bit, have some fun. She could see Tom continuing to twirl the axe handle, and the head of the axe spinning so fast, its whistling sound was deafening.

Tom was standing directly in front of her. There was nowhere to go. She had to do something and fast. Sara pretended to be out cold; the blood was pouring from her wound. Maybe if he saw the blood, he would not do anything just yet. Meanwhile, Sara's hand was busy under the bed, trying to find something, anything to defend herself with.

Tom walked over to where Sara was laying. He leaned over, grabbed her by the hair, and pulled her away from the bed along the floor of her bedroom. Suddenly he let go and raised his hand to his nose to smell the blood on his hand. Then he put one finger in his mouth and tasted her blood. He began to laugh—the most sadistic laugh Sara had ever heard. Suddenly, a cat's meow filled the silence, and Tom turned his head quickly. As his back was turned, Sara took her chance. Without thinking, she raised her legs up from the floor and aimed straight for the back of his knees, bringing him down. Tom fell directly onto his face, turned onto his back, and looked at her with those black eyes and half grin. As he stared at her, she became more scared than ever before.

Sara stood up quickly and landed one leg down onto his groin. Tom didn't even blink his eyes. Sara knew that because he felt no pain, he couldn't be human. When someone has gone mad, she remembered, he gets stronger, and it takes much more to bring him down. How could she do any damage to this man when he was trying to kill her? Tom was a big and very strong man. The cat seemed to distract him more than her powerful blow to his groin. But why? she thought. Why was that cat so concerning to him?

Sara took her chances and tried to get away, but he grabbed her ankle with a crushing grip and pulled her down. Kicking and screaming, she hoped someone would hear her. Her hand was busy trying to find anything she might hit him with. At last she found a shoe at the foot of the bed…a shoe with the two-inch spike heel. Sara remembered leaving the pair of them at the foot of the bed the prior night after going out with the girls.

Sara's arm came up. This was her chance to do some kind of damage. She aimed for his eyes. If she could blind him, he would have a harder time finding her, or at least that's what she was hoping for. Sara raised the shoe, and when Tom turned his head again to look for the cat, she planted the spike deep into his forehead. Not the target she was going for but nevertheless effective. He fell like a tree whose roots were severed, falling straight onto his face and planting the shoe deeper into his forehead. His body filled the entryway to her room.

Sara started to sob. She was sure Tom was dead, and it felt like her ankle was on fire from where he had grabbed it just minutes earlier. Tom was now blocking her from escaping, laying there with the shoe protruding from his forehead. His eyes were wide open and black as if nothing but pure evil lived inside. His mouth was wide open with those needle-like teeth frozen in a look of horror.

Sara tried to take a better look at his wound. She couldn't see any blood, and the wound was dry. The only thing she could see was what appeared to be brain matter oozing out around the heel of the shoe. The flesh was peeled back with jagged edges, and it smelled like it had been in the hot sun for a week. That smell made her want to vomit. She just wanted out of there, and fast.

Sara stepped over Tom's quiet body. She needed to see if she could get any response from him, so she kicked him in his shoulder. When she did, she yelled out in pain from the injury to her ankle. But Tom didn't move a muscle. Sara looked for any signs of life and saw none. When she reached down to touch him, his skin was cold as ice. She quickly withdrew her hand, the feeling of his skin creeping her out. Tears rolled down her cheeks, and it took everything she had to not scream out loud. Sara managed to get over Tom's body and limp into the living room to call the police.

"My neighbor is trying to kill me," she screamed into the phone. "Send me help fast, please! He tried to kill me with an axe, and he broke down my front door. Please, please come quickly!" Sara could barely get the words out; she felt short of breath, hyperventilating. When she hung up, she tried to calm down a little. Her life depended on it.

She realized she should have stayed on the phone, so she decided to call the police again. As she did, she slowly turned her head and looked at the bedroom doorway. Tom's body was gone! She heard footsteps; she turned toward the sound and there he was, wearing that scary grin. The axe had found its way back in his hand. He was twirling it as if he were telling her it was meant for her and only her…again.

She limped around the couch, trying to escape outside where she could wait for the police. That was her only chance. Sara grabbed a fireplace poker for protection and headed for the front door. Tom came toward her with the axe. It was resting on his shoulder as if he had just finished cutting wood, but she knew his work hadn't even begun, and it wouldn't be done until she was dead.

Sara swung the poker and struck him in the neck, the bones cracking on impact. His neck bones could literally move from one side to another. Tom gagged and seemed to have the wind knocked out of him. He dropped the axe, held his neck with both hands, and went down; the axe lay next to him. This time he would hopefully stay down. But she did not want to take any chances. Sara held the poker in both hands while straddling Tom. She raised it above her head and prepared to bring it down once and for all, making sure Tom did not get up.

The fear inside Sara was replaced by anger. She was mad that Tom came into her home and tried to attack her for no reason, turning her life upside down. First he made her love him and now this.

Sara started hitting Tom in the face, crying and yelling, telling him to stay down. "I'm going to make sure you never get up again," she cried, nearly hysterical now. "You're never going to hurt anyone ever again. I'm going to kill you!" Sara wasn't sure if Tom could die, so she continued to hit him with the poker from the fireplace, yelling, "Die, loser, die already! I'm going to make sure you never get up and hurt anyone again. Die, die already!"

Sara surprised herself with the degree of violence she was inflicting. When she was done, she barely recognized his face. Tom had blood coming from the multiple wounds she had inflicted. She was morbidly happy, and a creepy ease came over her as she looked at Tom lying bloodied and motionless on the living room floor. Sara could see the hole in the middle of his forehead where the shoe had once been.

Then Sara saw it ...movement. Tom was trying to get up, and the cops still hadn't arrived. Sara needed to get out of the apartment. As she ran for the front door, she felt that crushing grip around her ankle, the other one this time, in a grip even more powerful than she remembered. She fell to her knees and tried to get up, but his strength was overpowering. She turned and tried to kick him with her one free leg, and he finally let go. It felt like both of her ankles had been crushed, and she could barely stand on them. She knew Tom was going to make sure she couldn't get away. As Sara tried to stand up, Tom got quickly to his feet and blocked the front door, sensing what her next move would be. No, he wasn't going to let her out, not until he finished what he came to do, she was sure of that.

Sara remembered she had a gun in the hall closet that her dad gave her years ago for protection. She didn't know if it still worked, but she knew she had to retrieve it. Sara crawled to the closet and closed herself inside. She felt more vulnerable than she ever felt in her life, but if she could get the gun, she might have a better chance. Pulling down as many boxes as she could reach, she finally retrieved the gun.

She reached into another box, trying to remember if she even had any bullets. Tom obviously wasn't human, maybe the bullets wouldn't work, anyway.

She placed her ear to the door to see if she could hear any noises coming from the living room. She jumped when she heard someone knocking at the closet door, then walk away. She prayed it was the police, and got the feeling that whoever was out there was giving her permission to safely come out of the closet. As Sara began to open the closet door, she heard her name being called in a low almost whisper. Sara knew it wasn't the police. It was Tom. It wasn't safe in the closet anymore, and she wanted to be in the open when the police arrived. But she had no choice.

Tears were rolling down her face. The last thing she wanted was to be caught in such a confined space, but it was too late. Sara tried to cover herself up with some of the things she had hanging in the closet. She heard footsteps coming closer, and then leaving, as if he were pacing, waiting for her to come out. Then the doorknob slowly began to turn, but the door never opened. She stood as still as she could, trying not to breathe too heavily or sob too loudly. Holding the gun in her hand, she hoped and prayed Tom would leave her alone, not kill her.

Sara suddenly felt something crawling up her arm. When she looked down, all she could see was a large black figure. She grabbed it and, in the dim light peeking from under the closet door, she saw it was a large cockroach. She wanted to scream as she threw the bug off to the side. It took every ounce of strength she had to remain quiet.

Sara couldn't believe the police hadn't arrived. "Where the hell are they?" she yelled in silence, over and over, as tears streamed down her face. The closet was stifling, and she could barely breathe.

Then Sara felt a pinch and then pain…and then another and another. The cockroaches were biting her; she felt like she was being eaten alive. They were all over her. Sara bit her lip and tried to take deep breaths to keep from yelling. Sara could feel warm liquid running down her arms, down her cheeks and face, getting into her eyes. Sara began to scream out in pain. She heard Tom outside the closet door, laughing. In an evil tone that sent chills up and down her spine. He just kept laughing, and the cockroaches just kept biting, one after another. Every inch of her body hurt, and she felt blood running down her arms and soaking her pants and shirt. The harder Tom laughed, the harder and deeper the bites became. When Tom stopped laughing, the cockroaches stopped biting her. He was controlling them, but how? Tom was possessed by something so evil, she didn't understand it, and she didn't care. She just wanted to stay alive.

Sara got to her feet. She had the gun in her hand, and she was going to protect herself one way or the other. She ran out of the closet. Tom was standing off to the side, like he wanted her out in the open, and he still had that same half-moon smile that scared Sara even more than the axe in his hand. She felt like a deer running for its life, away from all the hunters. She might be easier prey out in the open, but she wasn't going down without a fight.

When she was almost at the front door, she turned to look back and saw the hole she made with the shoe and a very bloody face. She could barely make out that this person was Tom; there was so much blood, and his neck was still deformed. He looked to Sara like someone who had been lying in the grave for a long time. Black blood oozed from all the open wounds on Tom's face, and that smell, Sara had smelled it before, it was the smell of death.

Sara reached the front door and, in an instant, Tom was standing directly in front of it. She gasped, not knowing how he got there. But there he was, like a ghost, blocking her escape. Sara tried to talk to him as she slowly walked backwards, trying to put some distance between them. "Tom, why are you doing this?" she said. "What is wrong with you?" He just looked at her with that smile.

"Tom," Sara said, "why do you want to hurt me?" Once more, there was no response. Only that hideous smile.

Sara felt sick to her stomach. She knew what she was going to have to do to protect herself. She knew she would have to shoot him, but he seemed indestructible. She knew he wasn't human now, he was something else, and that evil smile told her there was nothing left of *her* Tom, wherever Tom was. He wasn't here in his body. No, this thing in front of her was something much more evil than any one person could ever be.

Sara tried to get around him, hoping he would chase her around the couch. He didn't follow her lead. Sara aimed the gun at his face and fired three times, but it didn't work. Click, click, click. No bullets, she thought, no bullets. She knew the only thing left was to try to run right through him. She took a running start, but it was like running into a brick wall. To her surprise, he fell over. She was on top on him, and then he rolled and was on top of her. He took hold of Sara by the shoulders and began to laugh. Sara tried to break free, hitting him in the head with the gun. Nothing. He felt no pain. He was strong but not quick. She managed to break free by rolling over and crawling toward the couch. When Sara tried to get up, she banged her right leg on a piece of broken door, and it impaled itself in the soft flesh of her thigh. Sara fell on her back in agony, but she rebounded and pulled the piece of wood from her leg. She didn't have time to bleed or have pain; she was fighting for her life.

Sara could see Tom getting up. She tried to get away, but between her ankle injuries and her bleeding thigh, she didn't get far before falling down. She felt doomed to die. She was tired and didn't have any energy left; Tom came toward her, the axe in his hand once again. She tried one more time to get up, but Tom pushed her down and kept her there. She was going to die, and she knew it.

Straddling her, Tom took hold of the axe with both hands and raised it up. In one last attempt to save herself, Sara took hold of the gun that lay next to her hip, pulled the hammer back, and aimed point blank at Tom. She hoped the gun would work this time, that there was a bullet somewhere in the chamber that would bring Tom down. She was going to shoot him right between the eyes.

"STOP! Tom, don't make me shoot you," Sara yelled in desperation. "You were the man I was going to spend the rest of my life with. Why are you doing this?" she said in a low and sorrowful manner. If he heard pity in her voice, she thought, he might take some pity on her. But he just kept staring at her with those black eyes and twisted smile, the axe raised directly over his head. Sara could hear a low humming, then a low but extremely evil laugh. Sara brought the gun up and placed the barrel between his neck and throat with the hammer pulled back. Sara fired one shot directly into Tom's mouth from under his chin; not really where she wanted it to go, but it would have to do. He went down, jerking his head up and then backwards, and he didn't move. Tom fell directly onto Sara. He felt like he weighed 300 pounds, and it took all of Sara's strength to move him off her. She was covered in blood and body tissue. When she got onto her hands and feet, she vomited. She could hear someone breaking down the front door and begin running up the hall stairs. Were the police finally here? Sara was able to make it to her feet just as the door to her apartment burst open. Sara held the gun in her hand as she turned to see who was there.

"Police! Drop the weapon!"

With their weapons drawn, they ordered her, but Sara wasn't fast enough. In a split second, the police fired one shot into her right hand. Sara screamed in pain, "Why did you shoot me? He's the one who tried to kill me. He came after me. I was just trying to protect myself. Why, why?"

The room was dead quiet. As the police looked around, they were stunned. The room looked like a massacre had taken place. Blood on the walls resembled what a painter might do with a can of red paint, waving a brush all over the room. The once gray carpeting was now stained red and had debris everywhere from the door and broken furniture. The room was so quiet, you could hear Sara's blood dripping from her hand and hitting the carpet.

Tom's body was limp. He was lying on her living room floor, finally dead. Her nightmare was finally over, or so she thought. Little did she know her nightmares were just beginning, one after another.

The last thing Sara remembered before she passed out was being put into an ambulance. The last thought she could remember was "How could an ordinary person start off having an ordinary day that turns to the most horrible night of her life?"

THE BEGINNING

Sara was 30, a very attractive woman who had accomplished a lot in her young hard life. Sara had long brown hair with radiantly crystal blue eyes. She was five feet nine and slender, and she made it a point to work out whenever she could. When Sara was a child, she was always told she should enter pageants, but she was too self-conscious and too busy trying to keep her family together.

She grew up in Chicago. Her parents, Bill and Ann, worked hard all their lives but never got very far. Sara could even remember being homeless a few times; Chicago had some very harsh winters, which were not very profitable for a construction worker. Her mom worked any job she could find, but she had a hard time keeping them because she was in and out of mental hospitals. Getting fired was a normal thing in her household. In between jobs, Sara's father tried to make sure Ann stayed healthy. It was very hard for Sara to have a normal childhood, always trying to take care of her dad, always moving from apartment to apartment, one rundown place after another.

Sara was a strange child according to her teachers, very withdrawn and too quiet for a child of her age. Her teachers voiced their concerns to her dad, saying all she ever wanted to do was read. They didn't feel that was normal; they felt she should be playing dolls and dress-up like other little girls. Once at parent-teacher conferences, they recommended that Sara have a psychiatric evaluation, given her mother's history. Instead they found out her IQ was in range of 160 and labeled her a genius.

In high school, she won many scholarships and chose UCLA in California. She wanted to go to school where the weather was always warm and sunny; she needed to get away from Chicago's harsh winters and boiling summers. Sara worked in local fast food places when she wasn't studying and managed to become a corporate attorney. She never wanted to do litigation in the courtroom; she felt she didn't have the killer instincts needed to practice that type of law. She also managed to earn her MBA. She got a job at a prestigious law firm and became one of its most productive attorneys.

She was thirty years old and looked like she was eighteen instead. She felt her coworkers had a hard time with her due to her age. Amid the typical rumors that she slept her way into her job, she felt she had to prove herself even more, work harder than anyone there. That's just what she did. She won many awards for her hard work and dedication, doing pro bono work at a local legal aid center. She felt like she had to give something back because she had received so much.

After saving for a few years, she decided it was time to buy her dream home. Her work was steady and stable, and she knew this would be a good time. She also wanted to get her parents out of Chicago and with her. Her mother was becoming more unstable as she got older, and her father was afraid she would go into a hospital and never come out. And both of them were getting up in years.

After looking at many homes, she decided to look at rental properties. She thought of practicality as well as profitability: Her parents could stay in one of the empty apartments and never have to worry about being homeless ever again, and she could live in another. Everyone could still have their space yet, still be close enough to see each other every day. Sara found this wonderful apartment building close to work. The two apartments on the top floor each had two bedrooms; the two on the bottom floor had one bedroom each. Sara would take one apartment with two bedrooms and convert one bedroom into a home office. The other two-bedroom apartment was already rented to an actress named Amber who was always away on movie shoots. Tom lived to directly below her in one of the one-bedroom apartments. The other one-bedroom apartment was vacant, and she would leave that for her parents.

The first time Sara saw Tom, she felt instantly attracted to him. He was tall, very muscular, and seemed very sweet. She felt it wasn't a good time to begin any kind of relationship. Then she realized you can't find peace by avoiding life, so she decided she would ask him out on a date…sometime. All she needed was the courage.

Now that all of Sara's apartments were rented, which helped pay the enormous mortgage every month, she could get her life going. She called her parents and told them her plan. She thought if her mom felt a little more secure in life, she might get better. Sara's mother was diagnosed with bipolar disease; she would stay deeply depressed at times and then not sleep for days. She also was a paranoid schizophrenic and had periods when she was psychotic. There were times when she wouldn't get out of bed for weeks. Sara remembered her mother's behavior as erratic, talking to herself, swearing people were following her and were out to get her. Sara had memories of coming home from school and being pulled into a closet by her mother, who ranted about people outside trying to kill her. Sara had an idea about her mom's condition when she was a little girl, but her parents always tried to hide it. Sara even spent time in a foster home because her father couldn't take care of her, and her mother was in the hospital. Sara just did what she had to do and dealt with it.

After several visits to the apartment building, she decided to make them an offer, which they took. Sara was in heaven the day she closed on her new property. She never felt so secure in her life. She made six figures a year, her job was secure, she now owned her own home, and she never had to worry about either herself or her parents being homeless.

The outside of the apartment building was white with black windows. It was once a large mansion; San Francisco was filled with mansions turned into apartment buildings. The entire building was newly remodeled with new carpeting, windows, and appliances. They had also recently replaced the roof and furnace. Everything down to the faucets in the bathrooms was new. The kitchens were remodeled with earth tone–colored appliances and fresh new paint. The bathrooms and kitchens had new tile. She wouldn't have to do much for a long time but enjoy the place.

The apartment building also came with a two-car garage and a half basement. When Sara took a walk-through prior to closing on the building, she noticed the basement room looked smaller than the upstairs, like something was missing. Sara noticed a large full-length mirror. Behind it was a door to another room. She figured that's why the space looked small, but she didn't ask to see the second room. She could check it out later.

This part of the basement had two washers and two dryers in one corner. The furnace was in another corner. It reminded her of a monster with a big mouth and flames coming out of it, but she knew she was just being silly. She remembered watching a movie where the furnace seemed to come alive and tried to eat the little boy until he ignored it and convinced him it was not real, so the nightmare went away, never to return. She thought about remodeling the basement to make it more comfortable.

Things really looked up for her now. Sara called her parents the day she closed. They said it would be at least a couple of weeks before they could make it out there, but they would come and couldn't wait to see her. Tom had even offered to interview her father for a job with his construction company. Everything was going beautifully.

THE MIRROR

After moving and getting her apartment straightened up and everything in its place, Sara could finally relax. She had several weeks of vacation and decided to use some of them to decorate and get things just right. She also set up her home office, so if anything urgent came in, she could take care of it. Everything she needed was right at her fingertips. She had full accessibility to all her files at work so she could do fifty percent of her work at home when she came off vacation. Her boss was so impressed with her work; he wanted to give her a promotion and a possible partnership. Something else wonderful to look forward to, she thought happily.

One day, Sara decided it was time to go downstairs into the basement and look behind that door that was hidden by the mirror. She had almost forgotten about it, except for the nagging feeling that something just wasn't right. Something bothered her about the way the door was hidden by that mirror. When she asked the realtor about the door, she said there was nothing in the listing about that room, and that it might just be a small storage area. Sara still felt uneasy about it, but at the same time, she was drawn toward that room.

Sara decided to do some laundry while she was down there, so she gathered her clothes and walked slowly down the basement stairs. She grabbed the flashlight she kept on the ledge at the top of the stairs. She definitely needed to put more lights down there, for everyone's safety. The old brick walls were also in need of serious repair.

After loading her clothes into the washers, she walked toward the full-length mirror. It looked very old and was about seven feet tall with beautiful wood carving of flowers and scary little fat faces of cherubs. The mirror reminded her of some of the antique furniture from the turn of the century. Something strange was happening—she felt like she was being drawn into the mirror, and she could almost swear it was calling her name. She swore it was illuminated with an eerie light. She was feeling very uneasy, as if someone was watching her, but she knew she was the only one in the basement. She had no desire to run away. She had to find out what was in that room.

Sara tried to move the mirror out of the way, but it wouldn't budge. The door looked solid and very heavy, too. Whoever placed the mirror in front of the door wanted to keep people out of that room, but why? Was something awful behind the door? She tried once more to move the mirror, to no avail. Sara decided to wait until Tom came home from work and gets his assistance, or she might have to hire someone to come and move it.

Sara was sitting on top of the dryer when she heard someone calling her name in a low, soft voice, "Saaraa…Saaaraaa." Sara jumped off the dryer and began to look around where she thought the sound was coming from, flashlight in hand. Sara was now feeling like she shouldn't be down there by herself. The lighting was so bad; she couldn't see all the corners of the basement well enough to feel comfortable, even with her flashlight. She was almost expecting for something or someone to jump out at her, like in the movies.

After ten minutes and not finding anything, she went back to the dryer and sat down. Sara was trying to figure out how she could make it more comfortable for her and her tenants to do laundry down there. She was thinking a couch, several chairs, some lamps, and a coffee table would really be nice. She could also put a TV down there and maybe some shelves for some reading materials. She could almost make it a recreation room for everyone who lived in the building, a place where they could throw parties. She wanted something real homelike down there. She could even have a small kitchenette area. Maybe she would even be able to do some work down there while doing laundry. She thought that would be so nice and convenient.

Outside it had begun to storm. Sara could hear the rain hitting the small few windows in the basement. Suddenly she heard a loud clap of thunder, which made her jump. Lightening flashes gave the room an even eerier look. The storm was getting really bad, and Sara was getting scared down there by herself. All she wanted to do was run upstairs, jump into her bed, and throw the blankets over her head like she did when she was a child, but she knew she was being silly. She remembered when she was eight and a bad thunderstorm hit. She ran and jumped into bed with her parents and felt safe and secure cuddling up to them as close as she could. The memory gave her a smile; it was one of the few she had that were really good. She could remember the feeling as if it happened yesterday. Sara had lived by herself for so long, she forgot how it felt to have the security of her parents. But that would soon change, and she was so happy about that.

A thunder clap jolted her back to reality. In horror movies, when you see someone in a basement and a severe thunderstorm hits, something always happens, nothing ever good, she thought. Just as that thought hit her, the lights began to flicker, the electricity threatening to go out due to the storm. She jumped off the dryer and restarted it. Maybe she should install an extra generator just for this purpose.

Suddenly she heard the basement door open, and she saw the light from the hallway at the top of the stairs. Just a peek of light at first, then a streak of light, and then she saw a shadow standing at the top of the stairs. Sara was barely able to keep from screaming. She jumped off the dryer and yelled out, "Who's there?" There was nothing but silence. Sara looked up at the door with much anticipation and anxiety. After what felt like ten minutes, she heard, "Hey, Sara, it's me." It was Tom.

"You asshole, you scared the living daylights out of me!" Sara yelled in a high-pitched, almost screeching voice. She was actually happy he was there but pissed that he scared the crap out of her.

"Hey, Tom, can you come down here for a second? I need your help really quick," Sara said, her voice now much calmer.

"Sure, what you need?" Tom said as he walked downstairs. When he saw Sara, Tom felt instantly attracted to her. In the dim light and sudden flashes of lightening, she never looked more radiant and beautiful. She was wearing jeans and an old T-shirt that was stained and had small holes everywhere. Even in that outfit, there was something about her that he wanted and needed badly.

Sara felt embarrassed by the way she looked, but she didn't care. Her appearance was always an issue with her. She hoped that sooner or later, Tom would ask her out and see her at her best. Now that he'd seen her at her worst, if he asked her out, she would know it was because he truly liked her.

"Tom," Sara asked, "can you help me move this mirror off to the side? I want to see what's behind the door that's behind this mirror."

Tom looked behind the mirror and exclaimed, "Wow! What's that? It looks like a door."

"Yes, genius. I just said, can you help me move this mirror from in front of the door." Tom just looked at her and laughed. "Smart ass, you're a smart ass, and so funny." Sara gave Tom a light slap on his arm.

Tom pushed on the mirror and moved it about two inches. "Damn, Sara, what's this made of, steel?"

"Yeah, I know it's heavy. That's why I needed your help," Sara replied. After several attempts and a lot of sweat, Tom was able to move it completely from in front of the door.

"Wow," stated Sara. "Thank you! I wonder why they wanted to hide this door."

THE SECRET ROOM

The door looked very old and was about six feet high by five feet in width. The top was curved with long planks that ran vertically. The door knob was a round O ring that was rusted and hard to turn. Sara then realized the door just pulled open, so she took the ring in both hands, placed one foot against the wall to brace herself, and pulled with all her strength. The door did not budge the first time she attempted to open it. She tried again, and the door budged about two inches. Tom helped, and together, they succeeded in opening the heavy door. Dust and debris flew everywhere, getting in Sara's eyes. She ran to the utility sink to wash out her eyes. Tom followed to make sure she was okay.

"Sara, are you OK?" he asked in alarm.

"I'm fine," Sara replied. "I just needed to wash the dust out of my contacts before they got scratched, but thank you for being so concerned, I really appreciate that. Obviously no one has opened that door in a long time. I wonder what's in that room that someone was trying to hide?"

Tom said, "We'll find out in a minute won't we?"

Sara took her flashlight and entered the room, Tom directly behind her. The room was dark and full of spider webs acting like a wall they had to clear a pathway through. The air was stale, stagnant, and full of dust, making both of them cough. Tom took the flashlight, aimed the beam around, and found an old pull chain in the middle of the room. When Sara pulled it, several Tiffany lamps became dimly lit. Their multi-colored flowered lampshades gave the room an eerie glow. An uneasy feeling came over Sara. Something about this room was completely wrong. She had the feeling this room was used for nothing but bad things. She could feel it in the pit of her stomach; the energy of the room was wrong. She could almost feel the evil pulsating through the walls.

Tom said, "I've been living here for two years and never knew this room existed."

Sara replied, "You probably just came down here to do your laundry, nothing else. I almost missed it when I came to see the place for the first time." Sara looked around and noticed a large wooden desk with a leather chair, both covered in what looked like two inches of dust. Two of the lamps sat on the desk, one to the right and one to the left, along with some old newspapers and large books, mostly scrapbooks and ledgers. Someone must have done business down here at one time. It looked as if that person had planned to come back and finish his work, but never did. A pair of what appeared to be very old men's glasses sat on top of the newspaper as if someone was reading the paper, became distracted, and laid the glasses down to rest his eyes.

Sara panned around the room with her flashlight. The walls were lined with bookshelves filled with hundreds of old and dusty books all covered in thick blankets of dust, dried bug carcasses, and spider webs. The floor was made of solid, uneven, dust-covered stones.

"Someone must have used this room has an office at one time," noted Tom.

"Yes, but it doesn't look like it's been used in years," replied Sara. She walked over to the desk and wiped away enough dust to read the date on the paper—April 1, 1905. She picked up the newspaper, and it nearly crumbled in her hand.

"Wow!" exclaimed Sara. "Look at this newspaper's date. It's like a hundred years old. I wonder if any of these books are worth anything." Sara turned to Tom with excitement in her voice, just like a child who hoped to find buried treasure on an island. "I wonder if there are any articles on, like, the Titanic or any other major things that might have any significance. They could be worth some money, you know." Sara went around to the desk and sat in the chair. She wanted to go through the drawers to see if she could find anything interesting. Sara could hear the chair's wood telling its age, wood splitting very low at first, then collapsing beneath her, landing her on behind. She yelled out in pain when she hit the floor, and the flashlight rolled under the desk. Tom turned and ran toward her. She was laughing and whining at the same time.

Tom began to laugh, asking, "Are you all right?"

"Yeah. I think I hurt my pride more than my backside."

Tom took Sara by the arms and lifted her to her feet, almost throwing her into the bookshelf.

"Careful, you. You're going to put me through a wall, you brute," Sara yelled as Tom began swiping some of the dust off Sara's her backside. Both of them started to laugh.

"Watch the hands, buddy," she warned with a smile. She was trying to flirt with him and hoped it was working.

Sara looked around on the floor for her flashlight and saw the beam of light shining from under the desk. She got on her hands and knees and reached for it. When she did, something furry brushed against her cheek. It was small and quick and made Sara scream in fright. She withdrew her hand and got up quickly, hitting her forehead on the ledge of the desk as she did. A wave of nausea hit her, and she felt like she was going to pass out. When Tom reached her, he noticed a large cut on her forehead. He also saw something running back under the desk.

"Crap, that's a rat!" Tom took Sara by the shoulders and walked her out of the room as fast as he could, given she was unsteady on her feet. He directed her toward the basement steps and sat her down. Then he ran over to the sink and found a clean washcloth from Sara's laundry basket. He wet it in cold water and placed it on Sara's forehead.

"Are you okay?" Tom asked again.

"I'm fine, thanks," Sara said in a shaky voice.

"Did you see what was under the desk? A rat, or I think it was a rat," Tom said. "It looked as big as a cat! That thing was huge! I've never seen a rat so big before and, doing construction, that says a lot."

"That must have been what brushed against my cheek," Sara said with a shudder. "I really didn't need to know how big it was. Just touching me freaked me out enough, thanks."

Tom replied, "It's probably been down here for a long time. That room has been shut up for years. C'mon, let's get you back to your apartment and clean up that cut."

Sara stood up and almost fell over. Her head was spinning so fast, she wanted to vomit with each and every step she took. Tom put his arm around her and led her upstairs. She appreciated his kindness and his support, and leaned on him the entire way. She was so dizzy; she had a hard time putting one foot in front of the other. When they got to her apartment, Sara could barely pull out her keys. When she reached to put her key in the lock, she noticed her door was already slightly open.

THE INTRUDER

"Tom," Sara whispered, "I think someone's in my apartment. I know I shut and locked the door before I went down the basement." Sara was scared; she wanted to make sure that whoever was in her apartment wasn't the person downstairs causing the screaming she heard earlier.

Tom told Sara, "Wait here and I'll go check it out and make sure it's safe." Seeing that she was still unsteady, Tom told her to go sit on the top step at the end of the hall and wait for him. Then he walked cautiously into her apartment;

he didn't want to get hit on the head or even shot. Tom hoped that whoever was in her apartment wasn't too desperate to cause bodily harm. In case he was wrong, he quietly took the poker from the fireplace, making sure not to knock any of the tools together to alert who might be in the apartment. Tom knew people who commit those types of crimes don't care about human life. They hurt you and do not even think twice about it as long as they get what they want, and don't have to work for it. Drug addicts sometimes do things they normally wouldn't. They hurt you for ten bucks if it means getting their next fix. This was the one thought that kept going through his mind. He didn't find anything on his search, but Sara's apartment sure did smell bad!

When Tom returned a few minutes later, Sara noticed a funny look on his face.

"What's wrong?" Sara asked from her perch on the top of the staircase; she noticed a foul smell that seemed to be coming from him. Sara stood up and almost fell over again, still feeling dizzy.

"Sara, nobody's there, but it smells like something's rotting in your apartment, like something died in there and has been dead a long time."

"What are you talking about?" Sara pushed Tom aside, entered her apartment, and quickly covered her nose. Her nausea returned and threatened to get the best of her.

"Damn! What is that smell? It's awful. What happened in here?"

Sara was holding her arm over her nose now, the smell was so horrible. Sara had never smelled anything like it in her life. It smelled like someone had put a rotting cut-off finger in each of her nostrils and left them there on a 95-degree day.

Tom and Sara walked through the apartment, finding nothing that would explain where that offensive smell was coming from. Sara began opening windows and turning on fans; she needed to rid her apartment of the smell.

After a few minutes of attempting to air out her apartment, the cut on Sara's forehead started to bleed again. Tom took Sara into the bathroom and got some disinfectant and Band-Aids. The smell seemed to get weaker; the disinfectant seemed to cover the odor of her apartment.

Awakened Dreams

After cleaning and dressing her wounds, Tom went looking all over again to try and explain the smell. After an hour of searching, Tom hadn't found anything. He asked Sara if she felt better, which she did, but she would feel even better if she could find out where that smell was coming from that seemed to invade every pore of her body. Tom invited Sara to join him downstairs, possibly for some dinner. He felt the need to watch over her, especially since she had a head injury. He even offered to take her to the emergency room—he felt she may need a stitch or two—but she declined his invitation. She just wanted to lay down for a while, smell and all. Tom told Sara he had to go downstairs to make some business calls, but he would be up in a little while and check on her. Sara told him that was unnecessary, and he told her he didn't care, he would check on her regardless. Sara felt better after Tom said that; she now knew he was interested in her.

"Thank you for all your help today," said Sara.

"Are you sure you don't want me to stay and search some more for the source of that smell?" asked Tom. He didn't know how she was going to lay down with that odor as strong as it was.

"At this point I could probably sleep in sulfur mines; I just need to lie down," she told him. "I'll worry about the smell in a little while; I'm feeling dizzy."

Tom suggested going to the emergency room again, and Sara told him not to be foolish, that she would be okay. Tom left, promising to return after he had made his calls, and Sara closed and locked the door behind him. When she turned around to go into the kitchen, she almost fell over what appeared to be a cat.

"Well, hi there," Sara said to the cat. "Where did you come from?" The cat was meowing and walking in and out of her legs, getting black, oozy stuff all over the bottom of her pant legs. The cat was white, but he was full of this black stuff that was sticky and smelled really bad. Sara tried to stay away from him. He appeared friendly enough; she just couldn't take that smell.

"Oh," Sara said, "you're the one stinking up my apartment. Where did you come from?" She reached down to pick up the cat and decided against it. She got a can of tuna from the cabinet, opened it and placed it in a bowl on the floor outside in the hall along with a bowl of water. The cat eagerly ate and drank while Sara went back into the living room to get away from that smell.

Sara called the local groomer and her veterinarian. She would have to get the cat cleaned up before she tried to find out who owned him. Ben, as she dubbed him, was in need of a serious bath; she also wanted a clean bill of health from the vet.

First Sara needed to lie down and try to recover from her early morning injury. She was still feeling dizzy and sick to her stomach, but it was getting better. She just didn't need that smell to bring back all her symptoms—and her breakfast. Ben stayed out in the hallway.

A TRIP TO THE PET STORE

Several hours later, Sara felt like a new person again; aspirin and ibuprofen were wonder drugs as far as she was concerned. She felt so good; she decided to take a walk. She also needed to buy some provisions for Ben. She didn't know how long it might be before she found his owners, or if she would ever find them. If she didn't, she would keep him.

After the groomers and the vet, Sara stopped at the local pet store with Ben at hand. She had planned to hit the pet store while he was at the groomers', which was right next-door, but he became too aggressive when she was not in the room, scratching and biting them. As long as Sara was in the room, he was cooperative.

At the pet shop, Sara got him a liter box, cat food, some toys, and a window box so he could hang around the window and watch the birds. She also decided to get him a cat tree house so he would be more comfortable and would have a place to play. The vet said he was a middle-aged cat, and he seemed very affectionate and playful. The vet gave him all his shots and said he was very healthy and should live for a long time. She was pleased to hear that.

Sara began walking home from the vet's and all her shopping while Ben sat quietly in the cat carrier Sara had bought for the journey. Two blocks away from her apartment building, she walked past an old three-story Victorian-style home with wood trim. It reminded her of an old haunted house you see in the movies. Always at the end of the street, dark and rundown, something bad always lived in those houses. The house made her feel as if it somehow belonged to the large mirror in her basement that hid the secret door. The carvings were magnificent, very detailed with cherubs and fancy wood flowerets, the same kind found on the mirror. The house must have once been a show place in its day, Sara thought, with its big windows, wraparound porch and intricate trim. The house was in need of serious repair, but whoever bought it could really fix it up and have a wonderful home.

As she scanned the outside of the house, seeing its possibilities, Sara thought she saw someone in the top middle window, just a shadow of a person. Probably nothing, she reasoned. Sara walked up the front walk, which she could barely see due to the weeds. It was obvious nobody had been there or tried to take care of the place for a long time. She thought what a shame to let such a nice house get so dilapidated. The sidewalk leading to the front porch was cracked and missing some concrete. Walking up to the front steps, she noticed that boards were missing from the front porch, and cobwebs seem to be the décor.

Ben was also getting very restless in his cat carrier. He began to scratch and hiss. The closer Sara got to the house's front door, the more upset the cat became, sticking his paws through the holes and scratching her, drawing blood. She tried to calm him down, but nothing helped. He just became more aggressive.

She found herself standing in front of the front door with its beautifully etched frosted glass and a full view directly into the entryway of the house. Sara looked into the door and only saw broken furniture in the hall and lots of cobwebs, and she knew nobody had lived her for a long time. Ben was getting so upset, he was reaching through the holes of the carrier and scratching her so intensely, she almost dropped him.

"Ouch. Stop it!" Sara admonished the cat as she turned and walked back down the front stairs, careful not to fall through the rotting floorboards. The rest of the way home, Sara tried to keep her many scratches from bleeding all over the place; she couldn't believe Ben got so upset. When she reached her apartment and let Ben out of the carrier, he ran and hid under her bed. Sara went into the bathroom and cleaned and dressed her scratches, then set up his litter box in one of her spare closets. When she showed him where it was, he just smelled it and purred.

Sara heard a noise and immediately jumped; it was her door buzzer. Sara walked over to the intercom system and hit the button. It was her delivery from the pet store. After fifteen minutes of hauling in her purchases and placing fresh canned food and water in Ben's new bowls, Sara turned on water for tea and went and sat down in the living room. Ben jumped into her lap. He purred as Sara stroked his fur gently, He smells so good and feels so soft, Sara thought. She couldn't remember ever seeing a cat with such lovely eyes, big and the bluest she had ever seen. She felt they almost spoke to her. He is such a beautiful cat, she thought, very loving and affectionate.

She looked down at him and said, "It's just you and me, I guess, for now. You found me, and I found you, but just to let you know, I get the bathroom first in the morning." He was looking directly into her eyes as if he understood her. He was purring loudly and lying on his back in Sara's lap, trying to swat her fingers with his paws. He was in such a playful mood, even after everything he had gone through. Sara could almost hear him say "OK" with his purr.

The teapot began to whistle, so she placed Ben at the other end of the couch and walked into the kitchen. He got up and was at her feet instantly. Sara was fixing her tea when she heard people coming up the steps. Amid the commotion, she could also hear bags banging against the wall, like someone was trying to carry too many up at a time. It was Amber coming in from her latest movie shoot. Sara opened her door as they got to the landing.

"Hi Amber," Sara said.

"Oh. Hi, Sara. These are some of my co-workers, Rich and Bill and Pam, and they were at my movie shoot with me. They're all actors and actresses just like me." Sara noticed everyone had at least three bags in their arms trying to come up the front stairs.

"Sorry, Sara. I would love to talk, but I need to get these things into the apartment. We'll talk later, okay?" Amber seemed out of breath as she tried to talk and hold on to the bags of luggage she was lugging. Then Ben came walking out of Sara's apartment,

"Is he your new friend?" Amber asked.

"I found him, or rather, he found me," Sara stated like a new mother with her newborn child in hand.

"That looks like the cat a lady down the street had, but I think she died a while ago. She used, to sit in her rocking chair with that cat on her lap, or at least it looks like the same cat. I remember that cat because it had very bright blue eyes, and I don't ever remember seeing a cat with such blue eyes, almost neon blue. I used to see her when I'd walk to the stores."

"Amber, do you know if she ever said anything about missing her cat, or maybe the family's missing the cat. Have you seen any poster up about a missing cat like this? I would love to keep him, but if he belongs to someone, it's only right I give him back," Sara said.

Amber shook her head. "No, I don't remember seeing any poster up about a missing cat, but then I really haven't paid attention either."

"Can you tell me about where you saw the lady—her address, a name, something?"

"It's the only pink house on the block," Amber said. "She used to sit in that old rocking chair. I'm sure you've passed by it on your way to the store. She was a real strange lady, really mean or something, never had a smile on her face, I said hi to her a few times, but she just looked away, and if you went near the cat when it was sitting in her lap, it would hiss and try to scratch you. But that can't be the same cat. Besides, she told once when she did talk to me that her cat was about 20 years of age. That was probably two years ago, and there's no way that cat could still be alive."

Sara replied, "This couldn't be the same one then; the vet said he was about seven or so."

"Maybe he had babies, and this is one of his sons," suggested Amber.

"Well, I see you have to get unpacked, so we'll talk later. Thanks." Sara turned to go back into her apartment.

Amber responded, "No problem, see you later. Wait! Sara, would you like to come over for a glass of wine or something... maybe in a little while?"

"Yeah, maybe later on after you get all your things put away?" Sara said with a smile. She loved hearing about other people's jobs and how things were done, especially the special effects.

Amber said, "On second thought, let's shoot for tomorrow instead; maybe get some take-out or something. All I want is to sleep right now."

"Sounds good. Bye, Amber," Sara said with a wave.

"See you." Amber turned and went into her apartment. Sara wasn't sure about her relationship with Amber. It seemed distant somehow, but she was hoping they would become friends. Sara didn't make friends that easily. Everyone who did get to know her thought she was a little odd or strange somehow. Sara always thought Amber was a little self-centered, but she figured all rising stars were like that. She knew someday Amber would be a big star, and she had some jealousy about that.

Several hours later, Amber was knocking at her door.

"What's up?" Sara said with surprise in her voice; she assumed she wouldn't see her until tomorrow.

"I just wanted to give you this month's rent and the next four months in advance," Amber replied. "I'm leaving at the end of the week for another movie shoot. I just got the call from my agent. I've been waiting to hear on this really good part, and I'm not sure when I'll be back. I just want to make sure you get your rent right away and don't have to wait. I know you have a large mortgage now, so I know you'll need this."

"Thank you, Amber, for being so considerate. I really appreciate it," replied Sara.

"Would you like to stay for a glass of wine?" Sara asked.

"Sorry, Sara," Amber replied, shaking her head. "The only thing I want right now is sleep. I haven't been able to lie down yet, but I'm on my way."

Sara asked, "When does your movie open?"

"Sometime next year," she replied.

"Please let me know when. I would love to go and see it," Sara said with a big smile on her face. Amber was the only person she knew who was actually in a movie; it was exciting to her. Sara's life was filled with men in suits sitting around big conference tables. She led a somewhat boring life compared to Amber's.

"I'll see what I can do about getting us tickets to the premier," Amber said.

"I would love that! Thanks a lot. Is there anything in your apartment like plants that you would like me to take care of while you're gone?" Sara asked her.

"No, I got rid of all the plants a long time ago, because I'm gone so much. Listen, what are you doing tomorrow? I was wondering if you were planning to do any laundry."

"No, I did all mine today," Sara said.

"Great! I have tons, but I don't want to hog the machines."

"No, feel free, go ahead. And if there's anything I can do for you while you're gone, please let me know. I'll get your mail and stick it in a bag for you so when you come home, it's all together."

"Thanks, that would be great, I would really appreciate that. Maybe I'll come over later for that glass of wine, maybe we'll have a girls' night after all. I think I'm getting my second wind," Amber replied. Amber wanted to make a friend in Sara, but Sara scared her a little. Amber didn't do well with people who were so smart; somehow she felt out of place. Quiet people also scared her, and Sara was too quiet. Amber usually hung out with the more wild kind of people, the ones who liked to party all night; she was definitely a night girl.

"Great! See you later then." Amber turned and went back toward her apartment, and Sara shut the door behind her. She knew this would be like all the other times when she met someone who said he or she would let her know about a night out. It always turned out the same—she would never get a call and be left behind. This happened a lot to her, especially in college when she was seldom invited to parties. It bothered her sometimes, but she figured it was for the best. That's why she did so well in college, graduating valedictorian. Even so, it still hurt being left out all the time. After a while, she just stopped wishing she could be like everyone else and just did her own thing.

Sara wasn't watching where she was going and almost stepped on Ben. "You really need to stop doing that, or one of us is going to get hurt," she scolded the cat.

Sara got a call from Amber, who decided to stay in tonight and sleep; they would have to do the girls' night out some other time.

IS THIS REAL, OR JUST A BAD DREAM?

It was early in the morning when Sara was awakened by a bad dream. She was still feeling depressed about Amber passing on the girls' night out. She had fallen asleep on the couch, after telling herself it was okay, but she knew deep down she was disappointed. She dreamed that she was married and was being beaten up by her husband. The dream was so real that, when she woke up, she could feel the burning. Sara ran her hands up and down her legs; she could feel strap marks and welts running up and down both her legs. In Sara's entire life, she couldn't remember ever having a dream that was so vivid.

When she lifted her nightgown, she noticed large welts on her back and some on her belly. They hurt so badly, she thought that maybe she had been fighting with herself in bed. Maybe she was dreaming of someone hitting her and accidentally hit herself in her sleep.

She was trying to come up with excuses, anything to try to explain the marks, to find the truth. But what *was* the truth? Was someone in the room last night? Was she drugged and assaulted? Did that person who she thought was in the basement come back? Was this a warning from him?

No, she thought, she just had a bad dream, and it got carried away. She must have dreamed she was getting beat up or raped and tried to fend off whoever was doing this to her. That's the only explanation for the marks. Sara heard about things like this happening.

Sara decided to take a hot bath and then walk down to that pink house to see if anyone still lived there. She wanted to make sure no one was missing her cat. The warm, soapy water felt so good, and helped ease her pain. Lying in the bath felt so good that she must have fallen back asleep. She dreamed of the past in that pink house, and could almost visualize people walking up and down the street, women in long shirts and holding umbrellas to repel the sun. People riding in horse-drawn carriages. In her dream, Sara was walking down the street and onto the front walk of the pink house, only now she was in the present. She could see modern cars actually driving past her, and she could feel the breeze moving her hair from one side to another, wrapping it across her face.

She noticed a woman sitting in a broken-down old rocking chair with a cat in her lap. The cat was dirty with black tarry sticky stuff; he also appeared to be full of blood or what she thought was blood. The old woman had her face turned away as if something else was distracting her or she was just ignoring her. Sara couldn't see what she looked like, she could only see the profile of this old woman, and something wasn't right. She was wearing a yellow and pink flowered dress with skin-tone stockings that made her look very old. On her feet, she wore black granny shoes with silver buckles and a one-inch wide heel. She was slightly overweight with white hair pulled up into a body of mess like a teacher's bun.

When the old woman turned toward Sara, she screamed. The old lady's face was purple, and strips of flesh were hanging from her cheeks, as if one gentle touch would make her face melt off her bones, exposing the facial bones and muscles. The old lady looked like she had been dead for some time.

The cat which was sitting in her lap looked exactly like Ben; but this cat was dirty and foul smelling. Sara couldn't understand how she could smell in her dreams, but she could. She could never forget that awful smell of death and decay. The old woman was petting the cat with her bloated, blue hands and cradling him in a sign that she loved him very much. The cat was very receptive of her petting and appeared to enjoy every stroke. The old lady's fingertips were black and with every stroke, her fingernails fell off, one by one, and got stuck in the cat's thick, sticky coat.

Sara put both hands over her mouth to muffle the sounds of her screams. She turned to run back to her apartment, but found herself in the old woman's living room. Was this another nightmare? Was she awake? Was she asleep?

Sara closed her eyes and hoped, when she reopened them, that she would be back in her bathroom in the hot soapy water of her bath. But when she opened her eyes, she was in the dark, dusty living room filled with broken furniture. She began to walk toward the front door and was drawn to the family pictures hanging on the walls lining the staircase going up to the remaining floors. Pictures of family members that were surely dead by now since the pictures looked to be very old. Sara began to walk up the stairs and one picture in particular caught her eye. It was of a young girl; she looked 14 to16 years old. Sara wiped the dust off to see if it was dated. A small golden plate at the bottom of the frame read April 1, 1900. The girl was pretty. She was wearing a sailor dress and had braids in her hair.

Sara got to the top of the stairs, walking slowly over the old wood so she wouldn't end up in the basement; she was even cautious in her dreams. Sara was heading for the third floor when the old lady appeared in the middle of the staircase. Sara screamed in terror, stumbled backwards, and ran as fast as she could for the front door. She ran outside and jumped over the old rotting stairs. She fell and rolled over onto her back, screaming out in pain as if someone in her dream would actually hear her. She looked down and saw that her foot was completely twisted. Her bone was sticking out the side of her ankle, and blood poured from the open wound. The pain was unbearable, searing up her leg, and she finally passed out from the pain.

When she awoke sometime later, Sara was lying in the front of that old house wearing her nightgown. She did not know how she got there. She looked down and both of her ankles were completely intact. The pain was gone, and she could walk with no problems. She walked back to her apartment, trying to remember what happened. The last thing she remembered while awake was getting into the bathtub. She must have been sleepwalking.

When Sara reached her apartment, she began sobbing as she walked up the stairs. She didn't understand what was going on in her life and why she felt like she was going crazy. Thank God her apartment was unlocked since she didn't even remember leaving it. The first thing she noticed was that awful smell again. She walked into the bathroom, and Ben started purring and rubbing against her legs. He was dirty and muddy again, and it looked like old blood on him, and he smelled like he had been eating something bad for a long time. The smell was overwhelming.

Sara's nightgown was full of dirt and whatever black stuff Ben had on him, and the smell was making her sick. She reached the just in time to let loose whatever was in her stomach. Sara then went to pick up the dirty cat with a towel and put him in the hall, but he ran under the bed.

"NO!" Sara yelled. "Don't go under my bed, please!" Sara got on her hands and knees to see if she could grab him, but all she got for her effort was a swipe of his paw across her cheek, superficial, but nevertheless painful. She pulled back, grabbed her cheek with one hand, and ran for the bathroom. Sara rinsed a washcloth in cold water and placed it on her cheek. Sara kept thinking to herself, this vacation is going to kill me. I'm sleepwalking, waking up with injuries when I think I'm sleeping, and getting scratched to death. Maybe I *am* crazy. I think I need to get back to work.

Awakened Dreams

Sara cleaned up her face and, decided she needed another bath; she was all dusty and sweaty. The smell coming from her and from Ben was unbearable. But first, Sara needed to get him out from under the bed. She didn't want him getting whatever was all over him onto her new carpet. She was going try to do some coaxing with food, so she went into the kitchen. She looked at the clock—it was 8:30 are ready. She must have been in that house for at least an hour. She put on a pot of hot water for tea, retrieved a can of tuna out of the cabinet and opened it, and Ben came running. Only this time, he was as white as he was after his groomers' visit, and the smell was gone as well. Sara stared at him, totally confused. She went to the bathroom and turned on the bath water. She took off her nightgown and noticed the smell was gone. As she lowered herself into the tub, she felt the most relaxed she had felt in hours. She lay there for nearly thirty minutes, drinking in the relaxation she was getting from her bath. When she finally got out of the bathtub, put a towel around her, and looked into the mirror, she screamed in horror. Her face was blue and purple, bloated, and strips of flesh were falling into the sink. Her eyeballs were floating in bony, fleshless sockets. Sara kept on screaming.

Suddenly there was a loud knock at her front door. "Sara! Sara! Are you OK?!" It was Tom. He was walking in and heard her screams. Sara ran for the front door and into Tom's arms, sobbing so hard she could barely catch your breath.

Tom held her in his arms and tried to calm her down. "Sara what's wrong?" he asked in alarm.

"I just thought I saw something, that's all. Something horrible in the mirror. I was dead, or looked like I was dead. Tom, I don't know what's going on with me. I keep seeing things and hearing things." Sara told Tom everything that happened, but she was sure he didn't believe her. Tom had concern in his eyes and compassion in his voice, but deep down, she knew he didn't believe her.

"Tom I'm not crazy!" she yelled, feeling very vulnerable standing in front of Tom.

Tom replied, "I believe you, Sara. You just have to take it easy."

"Easy? You want me to take it easy?" she yelled. "Things are happening here that I can't explain. How can I take it easy?" Sara walked away from Tom as she tightened her robe around her and fixed the towel on her head. She felt like he was patronizing her, making her feel like she was dreaming the entire thing up.

"Listen, Tom, I'll be fine now. I think it was just a bad dream, even though it seemed more real than any dream I've ever had, that's all. I don't need your help any more, thanks." Sara was very sarcastic in her tone; she was annoyed with Tom and his seeming inability to believe her.

"Sara, please don't be like that," Tom begged.

"It's okay, Tom, you can go back to your apartment now, and I promise I'll be fine." Just then Sara's teakettle began to whistle, and Sara jumped.

"Look at you," Tom said. "It's just a teakettle, and you're really rattled. Listen, it's started to rain, so I'm not going to work. Do you want me to stay with you a while?"

"No," Sara replied more calmly. "I'm fine. I don't need a babysitter."

"Sara, it's not like that. I promise. I just want to make sure you're okay."

"I do appreciate that, Tom, I do, but I don't need looking after."

"Okay, but if you need something, just yell."

In an attempt to leave things on a more normal note, Sara asked Tom about an electrician for the basement lighting situation. He said he would call his friend and get back to her when he found out when he might be able to come and do the job. After thanking Tom and reassuring him that she was okay, Sara made herself a cup of hot tea and took it into the bathroom with her. She took her robe off, wanting to look at herself again; she knew she wouldn't find anything, but she wanted to be sure. Sure enough, all the welts were gone, every last one of them. It all must have been a dream, she thought. She still had the scratch on her cheek from Ben, and her butt was still sore from falling out of the broken chair in the basement, but for the most part, she was mark-free. She didn't want to try to explain it; she was just going to accept it.

TOM'S BIG MISHAP

After Sara's third cup of tea, she felt a lot better, like she might regain control of her emotions and mind. Sara has always been a very responsible and reliable person, and for her to start going crazy now was just strange. She had worked so hard, for so long, finally getting the things she longed for in life. She would do everything in her power to stop whatever was happening. She somehow thought these things were connected to either that room downstairs or that pink house, or maybe both, but she was going to find out, and quickly.

Sara put on jeans and an old T-shirt, making sure she had extra batteries for her flashlight. She was going down into that room to see if she could find out anything. Sara decided she needed to keep Ben locked up so she placed him in the bathroom, door shut. Sara headed toward the basement, walking quietly so she didn't alarm Tom. She just needed to be by herself. She couldn't take his "is she going crazy" looks.

When Sara opened the door that led to the basement, she thought she heard something. The closer she got to the bottom of the stairs, the louder the noise got, like gurgling, like air being sucked into something it couldn't escape. To her horror, she found out what was making the noises. It was Tom. He was hanging from the pipes in the basement, a large rope around his neck. He was swinging and kicking out of control trying to get himself loose, both hands around the rope that was taking his life one breath at a time. But his frantic movements were only making the rope tighter.

Sara tried to lift him by his ankles so he could get the rope undone, but she wasn't strong enough. Sara began screaming for help, hoping someone would hear her, and scrambled around looking for something to cut the rope with. She finally found an old box cutter, as well as an old box to stand on. Sara kept telling Tom to stop struggling; it was only making the rope tighter. Tom did as he was told. His face was beet red, and his eyes looked like they were going to come right out of his sockets. She was finally able to cut him down. Tom fell to the ground, gasping for air, holding his neck, unable to speak, but alive.

"What were you doing? What were you thinking?" Sara yelled. "Why would you try to hang yourself? Stay here, I'm going to call. You need to go to the hospital right now!"

Tom kept shaking his head until he could finally talk, but it was hard to understand him. Tom couldn't get enough air into his lungs to create much sound.

Sara kept asking him why he would try to hurt himself, and Tom replied in a voice that was nearly a whisper and coughing between each syllable.

"I don't even remember coming down here. All I remember was lying on the couch to take a nap. Next thing I'm down here fighting for my life. I don't even know how I got up there. I don't know anything. I dreamed I tried to hang myself. That's when I found myself down here actually hanging."

"Something is going on here, and we need to find out what it is before one of us gets killed. We have both had dreams that are so vivid, they could kill." Sara helped Tom to his feet and back to his apartment. Sara went into the bathroom and got a towel, soaked it in cold water, and wrapped it around his neck.

"This should help with the swelling and pain, but if you start having problems breathing, I'm calling 9-1-1."

Tom just nodded his head, "Okay, no problem. Then I won't argue with you."

"Tom," Sara said. "I really should take you to the hospital now, you know."

"Yeah, I know, but I really don't want to explain this to anyone. And the cold rag is helping a lot."

"Tom, why don't you lie down and take a nap? I'll stay here and keep an eye on you."

"OK," replied Tom gratefully, "but just for a minute."

Tom slept for several hours. He seemed to be sleeping peacefully, so Sara went upstairs to check on Ben. He was fine; she opened the bathroom door, and he came flying out. When Sara went back downstairs to check on Tom, he was up and drinking a cold cup of water when she walked in.

"Oh, I'm sorry. I thought you might still be sleeping so I didn't knock," she said, hesitating in the doorway. "I didn't want to wake you up."

"No problem, come on in. I just got up, and I'm really okay, you know, except for the neck burn and massive headache."

Sara gave him some aspirin and ibuprofen. "Here, this should make you more comfortable."

"Thanks, but I don't know if I can swallow them."

"Try," she said. It took Tom several minutes, but he was able to finally get the pills down his very sore throat. He felt as if he had drunk Drano, the burning was so bad.

Sara asked in a concerned voice, "Tom, do you want to tell me what really happened today? Are you sure you didn't try to kill yourself, that it wasn't a dream?"

"No, Sara, I didn't try to kill myself. I don't know what's going on, just like you didn't know about your dream. And I want to figure it out, as soon as I can swallow again and feel like I'm more alive." Tom took off the towel, and Sara saw the rope marks around his neck.

"Oh," Sara commiserated, "that's going to hurt for some time. Hope you have something to cover that up with."

"Don't worry," Tom replied, "I'll find something."

"Are you sure it's okay for me to leave?"

"Yes, go, I'm just going back to sleep," Tom said with an assertive voice.

AND THE DOOR WENT BANG!

While Tom napped on the couch, she decided to go downstairs to the basement to check out that room and to see if she could find anything related to what happened with Tom, and with her. Flashlight in hand, all she could find was the box he used to stand up on, and the rope. Who put him up there? And if he tried to kill himself, how did he have the courage to stand on that box and just kick it over, knowing he was going to die?

She was thinking this as she opened the door to the secret room and stepped in. Just as Sara turned around, the door slammed shut with a loud BANG! that echoed off the walls, just like in one of those old scary movies. Sara tried to open the door, but it wouldn't budge. She began to bang and pound, yelling and pleading for someone to let her out. No one could hear her cries for help.

She could hear things scampering all around in the dark. She kept trying to catch them with her flashlight, but she kept missing. She knew what they were—rats—big ones, from the sound of them. After what felt like hours of banging and yelling, Sara sat in the corner, hoping her flashlight held out, and fell asleep. In her dream, a large man and women appeared. Both looked familiar to her; she had seen them somewhere before. Both were wearing funny turn-of-the-century clothing, but something new was in the picture. A little girl, maybe fourteen or fifteen, with braids and a sailor dress. They were in some kind of room or parlor. The large man appeared to be her father. He was yelling at her and beating her with a belt. She had marks and welts all over her body, and she was screaming and pleading for her father to stop, but he wouldn't. The mother had a grin on her face as if she approved of the beating.

The man was yelling something to the girl, something about her getting pregnant. Sara began screaming for the man to stop, but every time she pleaded, he became more enraged, and his movements more violent. Then he did something so mean, she couldn't believe her eyes. The man took a cigar and held it to the girl's arm, causing a round cigar burn. The girl was screaming in agony, and Sara knew she had heard that scream before.

The scream woke her up, and Sara tried to jump up to stop the man. He scowled at her and said, "If you know what's good for you, you'll sit down; this is none of your business."

Sara could only scream at him, "You're a monster, stop that, don't hurt that little girl."

Just then the man grabbed Sara's arm and placed the cigar directly on her wrist. Sara started screaming in pain. She couldn't believe she should feel such pain in her dreams. Or was this a dream?

Just then, the big wooden door opened, and Sara saw Tom looking around anxiously. She jumped up and ran toward him. "Thank God you're here!" she cried as she held on to him.

"Sara, what are you doing down here? I called your apartment for hours. Have you been down here all that time?"

"Yes. I came down here to check out this room, and the door shut behind me. I couldn't get it open." Sara fell into Tom's arms, shaking and crying.

"Sara, why were you screaming so badly?"

"Tom, I was locked in that room. I couldn't get out. The door wouldn't budge."

"Sara, when I came down here, the door was opened about three feet. You could have gotten out any time you wanted."

"No! I'm telling you it wouldn't open when I tried!" Sara stormed out of the basement, Tom right behind her.

"I believe you! I'm just saying I heard you screaming, and I walked in and you were huddled in the corner."

Sara turned toward Tom to respond, and noticed something odd: The marks on his neck had disappeared. Sara looked at Tom with confusion. She began walking around him with her flashlight, aiming a beam of light directly at his neck. "What are you doing?" he asked with a confused look of his own.

"Tom, how's your neck feeling?"

"It's fine, why do you ask?"

"Well, because of what happened earlier," Sara replied with a hint of sarcasm in her voice.

"What happened earlier?" Tom was really confused now.

Sara turned toward Tom with a concerned look. "You know, when you were hanging from the pipes in the basement!"

"Sara," Tom exclaimed, "what are you talking about?"

Sara gestured toward the ceiling. "Tom, just a few hours ago, you were hanging from those pipes by a rope around your neck. Don't you remember?"

"No, I don't have any idea what you're talking about."

"Tom, I cut you down. You don't remember that?"

"No, Sara, I honestly don't."

Maybe I was dreaming, Sara thought as she looked away from Tom. Maybe I was having another nightmare, but it felt so real. I must have hit my head harder than I thought on the desk. Sara went upstairs, leaving Tom bewildered and standing in the basement. She needed some alone time, and she couldn't be around him at that particular moment.

An hour later, she decided to go back down by Tom's, and see if she could just forget this day ever happened. She had to try to explain herself to Tom before he really thought she was a nut job and never talked to her again. The wound on her wrist had disappeared, leaving her more confused now than she was earlier. Sara began to cry. She didn't understand what was happening to her, and she wasn't sure she wanted to know. She wondered if anything she had used to take care of Tom's wounds earlier was still visible. When she entered his apartment, it was spotless.

Tom asked her to stay for dinner. She really didn't feel like being alone right now, so she accepted his invitation. Maybe things would get better if she wasn't alone. Tom suggested Chinese take-out, which sounded good to Sara. She asked if he had any wine, he said yes, in the fridge.

"Yes, in the fridge," he said. "Set out some glasses, and I'll be right back with food. What do you like?"

Sara replied, "I don't know, surprise me."

"OK, be back in twenty minutes." Tom left, and Sara poured herself a glass of wine. She really needed it after the day she was having.

At the restaurant, Tom decided on a little of everything since he didn't know what Sara liked. As he headed back and passed the old pink house, he felt drawn to it. Tom stopped in front of the house and thought someone waving to him and calling his name. It looked like a little girl, and she was standing in the front doorway. Tom slowly walked up the decaying wooden steps and placed the bags of food on an old white rocking chair on the porch. Tom came to a large glass door and knocked.

fear, not only about the near-miss but about the events that just occurred.

When Tom returned about forty-five minutes later with the food, Sara noticed something different about him. The tone in his voice was a different pitch, somehow more shaky than usual. His face was pale, and he was sweating as if he had been running.

"What took so long and why are you covered in food?" Sara asked.

"I had a little accident, and I had to go back and get replacement food," Tom answered.

"Well, I got a head start on the wine part without you," she said, trying to lighten his mood.

Tom looked over and noticed half a bottle of wine gone. "I can see that."

"Go hop in the shower. I'll put the food out on the table."

"Sounds good to me," Tom said. He looked shaken up and as pale as a ghost. Sara asked him again what had happened.

"Nothing happened," Tom insisted. "I stupidly wasn't watching where I was going and walked into the street and a

Tom kept yelling, and finally the large man looked at him. Tom could see something in his hand—an axe. Tom turned and tried to run out of that house as fast as he could, but he tripped and fell into his bags of food on the rocking chair. He was covered in noodles, and the floor was covered in sauce, making it hard to regain his footing. When he managed to get up and head for the sidewalk, the large man blocked his way.

"Mind your own business," he warned. "Stay away from here if you know what's good for you." Then he brought the axe straight up and down, slicing Tom in two, but the axe was transparent. Tom looked down and saw the axe planted right into his belly, but it didn't hurt him. Then the man disappeared like steam coming out of a pot and rising to the ceiling. Tom quickly looked to see if the woman was still there, but she was gone, too.

He looked down and saw he was covered with Chinese food. Crap, he thought, I have to go back there, and I look like I've been in a garbage can. He wasn't paying attention where he was going while he was scraping noodles off himself. He realized he was in the middle of the road when a car sped past him, almost hitting him. Tom jumped out of way in and ripped up, with broken and missing legs, were strewn everywhere.

Tom decided there was nothing here he wanted to see doors he turned to leave and was nearly knocked over by a very large man standing in his way. Tom was so startled, he fell backwards, but quickly got up.

"Hi," Tom said. "I'm sorry for just coming in like this."

No response. Something wasn't right about him. Tom thought he could almost see right through him as if he were transparent. This large man didn't even look at Tom. A woman also appeared right in front of Tom, sitting in one of the broken chairs that seemed to repair itself right in front of his eyes. The large man walked over to the women and slapped her so hard, her hair came unraveled. Tom screamed at him to stop, but the man never even turned to look at him. Tom felt helpless. He couldn't do anything but watch as this large man began to beat this woman, He kept yelling, but no response. Tom felt like he was stuck in their world, and they were stuck in his. They were all stuck together, not realizing they could see and interact with each other. An imaginary wall divided them, but it was transparent.

THE MAN WITH THE AXE

"Hello," he called. There was no response. The house looked empty and unkempt; no one had lived there for years. Tom could barely see through the cobwebs that invaded the doorway. When he turned the doorknob, he found it was unlocked, so Tom entered the house with caution, clearing away cobwebs as he walked. The dust was so thick, he began to cough, and he felt like his lungs were going to explode. Tom came to what appeared to be a parlor or sitting room. Old furniture lined the walls. Chairs with fabric on the seats, old car almost hit me is all. I'm OK. Put the food on the table, and I'll be out in a minute. I'm just a bit shaken up, that's all. I'll be fine after a shower."

Tom reached over and kissed Sara on the forehead. She couldn't believe he did that and couldn't wait for him to do that again.

"Well, if you're sure you're OK," Sara replied with a happy smile on her face.

"Really, don't worry about me. I'll be out in just a minute." Tom took a shower and put on fresh clean clothes. When he emerged from the bathroom, Sara had the table set with dinnerware and wine glasses. They enjoyed their meal and each other's company. After cleaning up the dishes, they sat on the couch. They felt their attraction to each other without saying anything, not one single word.

Tom reached over, gently pulled Sara toward him, and kissed her. She felt so good in his arms, so soft and sweet smelling. All he wanted to do was make love to her, right there on his couch. They ended up doing just that for hours, not able to get enough of each other. Afterwards they just held each other before making love several more times. Sara wasn't sure where she was getting all this energy, but it didn't take much. Sara felt so wonderful when she finally fell asleep in Tom's arms. She had never been with a man so intensely before. She knew she was falling in love with him, and it was a good feeling. Tom was intense with her, yet so gentle, she felt like crying because of her complete happiness. Life was wonderful again.

Sara got up before Tom and peeked out the window. It was a rainy day. Sara decided to make breakfast; she was starving after the night's events. Sara walked into the kitchen and opened the fridge. Nothing, not even a tea bag. Sara got dressed and headed to the store, umbrella in hand, to pick up some things so she could fix breakfast. She did her shopping and was heading home carrying four bags when she passed the pink house and just stopped, dead in her tracks. She felt like some force was pulling her, like an invisible rope around her waist, but she resisted. Sara wasn't going back anywhere near that house after what happened to her the last time she was there. As Sara stood there and stared at the house, she thought she saw someone in the front window, a man. She remembered him, and she had no intention of intentionally meeting up with him again. It took everything she had to turn and keep walking toward her apartment building. She broke whatever grip that had on her and walked as fast as she could all the way back to Tom's door. Tom was up and making what little coffee there was in the house.

"Hey, where did you go?"

"I ran to the store. I thought you were sleeping; I was going to make you breakfast."

Tom went over to Sara, kissed her, and took some of the bags from her arms. "I'll put these things away. Why don't you go put some dry clothes on?"

"You're worse than me when it comes to no food in your house; your cupboards were bone bare."

"I know. I didn't get a chance to get to the store. You know, you remind me of something"

"Yeah? What's that?"

"A drowned rat."

Sara playfully whacked Tom on the arm. "Very funny! I'm a freezing drowned rat, so I'll be right back." Sara went to her apartment and selected a T-shirt and pair of fleece lounging pants. When she returned to Tom's apartment, breakfast was on the table.

"Tom," Sara said, "I was going to cook for you."

"Well, I beat you to it."

"It smells delicious; thank you. How about a fire to go with it?" Sara suggested. "The fireplace still works, doesn't it?"

"It should," said Tom. "I'll just go downstairs and grab some wood."

THE HAMMER

Tom wanted to start a fire for his drowned rat, so he headed for the basement door, slowly walked down the steps, and easily found the woodpile. As Tom knelt down to pick up some wood, everything went black.

When he woke up, he felt something warm running down the back of his neck. Tom felt like he had been beaten about the neck, and his head was swimming. He had the worst headache of his life. When he tried to stand up, the room went dark for a minute, and he sank back down to the floor, nauseous and stunned.

After a few minutes, Tom was able to slowly get up using the wall as a brace. He looked around to see what might have fallen and struck him in the head. The only thing Tom noticed was a hammer next to the woodpile lying in a small pool of his blood. Tom looked up and did not see a shelf or anything the hammer might have fallen from. He stumbled back to his apartment, slowly creeping up the basement stairs, trying not to fall from his dizziness.

Sara was coming out of the bathroom after blow-drying her hair and saw Tom stumbling toward the couch. She saw blood on the back of his shirt and on his hand where he had held his head.

"Tom, what happened?" Sara said in alarm as she ran to help him sit down; Tom was very unsteady on his feet.

"I went downstairs to get firewood and something hit me in the head, that's all. I think it was a hammer. There was one next to where I was laying, and it looked like there was blood on it."

"Are you sure?" Sara asked.

"Yes. A simple accident, no ghosts around. Maybe I knocked it down without realizing it when I reached for the wood."

"Let me take a look at your wound." Sara began touching Tom's head in an attempt to see how seriously he was hurt.

"It's really nothing," Tom said, gently pulling away and removing Sara's hand.

"Please let me look at it. I'm worried about you!" Tom relented. Sara saw he had a small laceration to the back of his head that still oozing blood.

"Tom, let's go to the bathroom so I can at least clean your head up," Sara said. "You do not know where or who was using that hammer last."

Tom rubbed his forehead, a confused look on his face. "I don't even remember ever seeing a hammer down there before, do you?"

Sara didn't seem to hear him in her preoccupation with his injury. "Tom, you really need to go to the emergency room and get checked out. I think you need stitches."

"No, really, I'm fine. Sara. I'll be OK," Tom reassured her. "It's just a small cut and looks worse than it really is. We just need to stop the bleeding, that's all."

"You still need to be looked at. Did you pass out?" Sara asked as she got some antiseptic and cotton balls and started cleaning the cut.

"Yeah, I think so, but I don't know. I don't even remember being hit, but the hammer was on the ground when I came to, so I assumed that's what got me."

After a moment, Sara stated, "Well at least the bleeding has stopped, so maybe you don't need to go to the hospital. How do you feel, Tom?"

"My head is really starting to hurt, and I'm nauseous."

"Let's get you back to the couch, and I'll get you some ibuprofen," Sara instructed as she started leading him back to the living room. "And take your shirt off so I can soak it in cold water to get the bloodstains out."

Tom did as he was told, though he wasn't sure if he could keep down the medication. Sara encouraged him to at least try; he would feel better in the long run.

Tom took the pills from her, looked her in the eye, and asked, "What do you think really happened, Sara?"

"I don't know," Sara replied. "But if you wanted attention, all you had to do was ask!" Sara was trying to make Tom smile and to lighten up the room a bit. Too many bad things had been happening, things no one could explain, and she was scared. But she was also happy that she and Tom had grown closer. She wanted to hold on to that happiness, at least for the day.

Tom lay on the couch, and Sara placed a quilt over him to keep him warm. She made herself a cup of tea and started a fire with the few pieces of wood Tom had in the apartment. They fell asleep in front of the fire in each other's arms. Sara dreamed. No nightmares, no killings, no injuries. Just sweet dreams of her and Tom.

When they woke up several hours later, both Tom and Sara had stiff necks and backs. Tom had an awful headache, and Sara suggested more over-the-counter pain medication, which Tom accepted eagerly. Sara told him to go lie in bed and take another nap while the pain medication kicked in. Tom instantly fell asleep again. He really wasn't feeling well.

He was pale and had a drawn look to his face, as if he was going to vomit any minute. Sara knew he needed to see a doctor, in spite of his protests to the contrary.

She decided to stay for a while and keep an eye on him. She remembered reading that you should wake people with head injuries every four hours to make sure they didn't have a concussion. After several hours passed and Tom had not woken up, Sara started to become concerned. She woke him up, and he easily aroused, his headache still present but better.

Sara decided to go to the basement and check things out for herself. She also wanted to go into the secret room again. She knew she could leave him for another four hours without harm. Sara began putting her shoes on when the phone rang.

THE VOICE

"Hello," Sara answered. There was no response. She repeated herself. Still no response. She hung up the receiver and continued to put her shoes on. The phone rang again, and she answered, "Hello."

A voice on the other end said to her in a deep voice that was definitely male and older sounding, "Mind your own business and don't go searching for things that don't concern you." Click. The phone went dead.

Awakened Dreams

Sara held the receiver in her hand. She knew she had heard that voice somewhere before; she just couldn't remember where. After sitting there for several minutes trying to remember, she gave up.

THE BATHROOM SCENE

Sara left Tom's apartment and was headed for the basement door when she noticed a terrible odor that seemed to be coming from the upstairs apartments. She slowly walked up the stairs, opened her apartment door, and found that the offensive odor was coming from her apartment. Sara slowly walked around, looking for anything that would tell her what the smell was. When she came to her bathroom door, the small was so bad, she felt nauseous. She began to gag and cough, feeling the burning deep in her lungs. Her heart was pounding and sweat began to roll down her forehead.

Sara firmly grabbed the door handle and slowly opened it to reveal the largest cockroaches she had ever seen. There was also a black cloud of bugs flying everywhere. In the bathtub, Sara could see a decomposing partially mutilated body. Snakes and cockroaches were slithering in and out of pockets where flesh used to be.

Sara was horrified and began to scream when she saw Ben sitting on the chest of this decomposing body. Ben it was chewing on something that looked like a strip of flesh, and he was covered in that black, sticky substance again. It looked like blood beginning dry in big clots in his fur. She quickly slammed the bathroom door shut and held firmly onto the doorknob as Ben scratched and pushed against the door trying to get out. The door bounced back and forth under his weight; it felt as if the cat weighed 50 pounds. He was hissing and meowing at the same time, and Sara could barely keep him from escaping.

Sara began to yell for Tom, who awoke to her screams and headed unsteadily up the stairs. Tom found Sara in her apartment holding tightly to the bathroom doorknob and looking terrified.

"Sara, what's going on?" Tom demanded.

"Don't go in there," Sara yelled.

"Sara," Tom stated, "let me see what's in there."

"No!" Sara yelled.

"Sara, please let go of the door handle." Tom tried to move Sara away from the door so he could investigate the source of her terror, but she refused to budge, still holding tightly to the doorknob with both hands in a panicked state.

"Sara, you have to let me see what's in that room. Please! Let go!" Tom was now nearly yelling at her, and she decided to let go of the door handle. She turned and slowly slid down the wall to the floor and rested her head inn her hands.

Tom opened the door slowly. Nothing, except the faint odor of freshly turned-over dirt. Tom barely noticed the single fly in the bathroom. Every house had a fly or two. Nothing to be alarmed about.

"Sara," Tom said, "there is nothing here. Your bathroom is spotless. What did you see?"

Sara turned and looked into the bathroom and couldn't believe her eyes. "Tom, I swear there were bugs crawling all over a dead body in the bathtub. You have to believe me. It was horrible."

"Well, Sara, whatever was here is now gone," he replied gently, helping her up from the floor. "Were you having another nightmare?"

Sara walked into the bathroom and gazed around. "I don't believe this! Just a minute ago, this bathroom was full of bugs and a dead body."

Tom looked at Sara. "Is it possible you were just sleep-walking? Why did you come up here?"

"I was going to go down the basement and check out some of those old books after I took a shower and put on a fresh change of clothes," Sara replied in an annoyed voice. She wasn't sure what to make of anything anymore.

Sara noticed sweat beginning to roll down Tom's forehead. His face looked gray, and he was swaying a little. Sara walked him to the couch and sat him down.

"Tom, you need to lie down." Sara was convinced she should have taken him to the emergency room, no matter how much he complained or protested. She needed for him to stay healthy. She felt as if she was losing her mind, but she knew she needed him by her side.

"Sara, I'm OK, really." Tom tried to sound convincing, to no avail.

"Yeah, you really look OK." Sara knew he was just trying to make her feel better. "You can't even stand for 20 minutes. You really need to see a doctor."

"Sara, no! I am OK. Just let me get my balance and the nausea will go away. Really! I must have gotten hit harder than I thought, that's all."

"Please Tom, go lay down in my bed," Sara implored him. "I really need to keep an eye on you for at least a little while longer. Please! I'll feel better if you at least let me do." Tom laughed and did as he was told. As soon as Sara was sure he was fast asleep, she headed down to the basement.

THE DIARY

Sara went through some of the papers in the desk first, not finding much of anything, just some old business papers, ledgers, newspaper articles, and the like, mostly from the 1910s. She felt like a kid in a candy store. She loved reading about the past.

In the last large drawer of the desk, she came across a diary. The name on it was Polly Mills. Sara opened to the first page—March 10, 1895. It was Polly's wedding day. The first few pages listed things she received as gifts and who gave them to her. It was a long and extensive list; she was obviously well liked in her time.

It appeared in writing that Polly led a normal married life. She liked putting down in writing her daily thoughts and things she needed to do, as if her diary were also a planner. She wrote down things such as dates for dinner with her friends and family, vacations she and Henry took. The last few pages contained rows of names and money amounts. Another row appeared to be birth dates with ages and then numbers in weeks, which Sara found odd. Was this something they donated to a charity or was it money they owed? What about the columns with the weeks? She couldn't figure it out and set the diary aside for later.

She started going through the rest of the books down there. By the time she had finished, there was a large mound of discarded books in front of her. She had turned each and every one of them up and over and found nothing. Sara wasn't sure exactly what she was looking for, but she knew something was there, hidden in some kind of code in the books.

In the last book she picked up, she found a wedding picture. On the back it read "Polly and Henry. March 10, 1895." Henry was a very large man, and Polly was small. What an odd-looking couple, she thought. She knew she had seen both of them before; she just couldn't remember where. Polly didn't look that happy in the picture, considering it was her wedding day. Henry had a mean-looking face with features that seemed cold and disapproving, especially his eyes, and his smile scared her somehow.

Sara was getting very frustrated with the whole thing, and with all the creepy things that were happening to her. All she wanted was answers. She knew she wasn't going to find them today, so she gave up and went upstairs. Tom was still fast asleep. She didn't want to wake him, but she wanted to make sure he was okay. She gently woke him up and asked him how he was feeling. He said he felt better, and his headache was finally going away. A happy and relieved Sara lay down beside him. Tom cradled her in his arms, and they both fell asleep.

Sara fell into a deep sleep and found herself back at the turn of the century, wearing the same kind of clothing she seen in the wedding picture—a long skirt and a large rimmed hat, holding an umbrella to keep the sun off her pale skin. Polly was there. She was a lovely woman with blue eyes and brown hair wrapped in a bun with delicate curls flowing down her face. She was quite stunning, yet Sara thought there was something very wrong about her, though she couldn't quite put her finger on it. Maybe it was her smile, a half-moon, and evil-looking somehow. Sara felt creeped out even in her dream. She just knew that somehow this woman was evil and so was her husband Henry, she just didn't know why she felt that way.

Sara woke up and sat up in bed. She looked around, saw Tom beside her, and immediately went back to sleep. In her next dream, she saw a woman wearing what appeared to be a wedding dress, and she was walking toward her in her dream. When she got close to Sara, the scene changed. With each step the woman took, the color of her face changed. It appeared to be turning black and became bloated. Then the flesh on the woman's face started peeling off, inch by inch, as if an invisible person was cutting her face with a razor. Sara could see each cut being made, exposing muscle and bone.

The white wedding dress began dripping with red blood. Sara watched in horror as her eyeballs fell out and maggots appeared in her eye sockets, finally covering her entire face.

Sara woke up screaming, sweat pouring from her entire body, and her heart was pounding so hard she couldn't catch her breath. Tom was still sleeping next to her. Sara looked over at her clock; she had only been asleep for an hour. She got up and headed for the bathroom. She walked cautiously through the very dimly lit apartment. Sara had pulled all the blinds down and drawn the curtains to help Tom with his headache which left the apartment dark as night. She also didn't want to step on Ben, who had a way of getting around; he even appeared at Tom's place several times.

Standing in front of the bathroom door, Sara took the doorknob in her hand, held her breath, and slowly opened the door. Sara could smell dirt and decay, so she decided to open the door just enough to stick in her hand and reach around to flip on the light. When she did, she felt something begin to crawl on her hand and quickly withdrew it when she felt a hand on her shoulder. She spun around, expecting to see a black bloated hand, but it was Tom.

"Can't you make some noise when you come in a room? You scared me to death!" Sara took a few deep breaths and tried to calm down.

"I heard you scream, so I decided to get up and make sure that you were okay," Tom said. "I didn't mean to scare you." He put his arms around her. "Man, you're soaked and shaking. Are you sure you're okay?"

"Yeah," she replied in a shaky voice, holding on to Tom a little tighter. "I had a nightmare and woke up drenched."

"Sara, why are you standing here? Were you sleepwalking?"

"No. I wanted to splash water on my face, but I couldn't go in," she said. "With everything that's been going on here, I'm afraid to just enter any room in my own house. I'm afraid things will jump out at me, or die in front of my face."

Tom cradled Sara in his arms. "I promise I won't let any more things happen to you, okay?"

Sara gave him a gentle kiss on the lips. "I love you," she said. She wasn't sure if she should say that since they just began dating, but the moment felt right, and things were moving on the fast side. Sara always had a way of rushing into a relationship and then getting her heart broken.

"I love you, too," Tom said, happy to know Sara felt the same way he did. He hadn't felt that way about anyone in such a long time, it put an enormous smile on his face.

Tom let go of Sara and went into the bathroom. She went back to bed and soon they were in each other's arms again. Sara felt a wall had been removed, the one wall that seemed to stop a lot of her relationships, those three little words. No nightmares when she fell asleep this time, just dreams she didn't remember, the kind she liked. Several hours later when they woke up, she made some sandwiches for dinner, ham and cheese with some chips and pop. Not very romantic but filling. After watching TV for a while, Tom decided he needed to go back to his apartment and do some payroll and business stuff. Sara kissed him and told him she would see him later. He kissed her back and told her he loved her.

Sara asked, "Will I see you after work tomorrow?"

"Yes, it's a date." Tom pulled her toward him and gave her another longer kiss, the kind she loved from him. This kiss made her tingle all over, and she did not want him to leave. In reality she knew he had to go home, and Ben was most certainly waiting for her and his dinner, meowing loudly in the other room.

"I'll cook us a nice dinner tomorrow. Don't work too long tonight; you're still recovering from your little accident," Sara said. "I love you, and I'll see you tomorrow."

When Tom left, Sara had a large smile on her face.

DINNER AT AMBER'S

Sara went back inside to feed Ben, do the rest of the dishes, and clean up a little. An hour later, she headed down to her parents' apartment. She had just had some furniture delivered and wanted to rearrange it so it looked nice. As Sara walked down the stairs, she ran into Amber coming up.

"Hey, Sara, how are you?"

"Great, Amber, how are you?"

"I'm tired but OK. I start my new movie in a couple weeks."

"Wow! Do they give you any time off?"

"Yeah, but if you want to make it in Hollywood, you have to stay active," Amber replied. "Got to stay where everyone can see you so they remember your name, but I really do love it. I really don't mind the time away and the hours. This is what I dreamed of for a long time."

"Yeah, you look like you're enjoying your career. You have to enjoy it or you shouldn't do it," Sara said with a smile on her face.

"Hey, Sara, why don't you come up for a glass of wine?" Amber suggested. "I just picked up some soup from this little restaurant around the corner. They have the best soup I've ever tasted, and I have plenty of both of us."

"OK. I'll be over shortly. We'll have that girls' evening. I want to know how a big film star gets treated on a big budget movie set."

"That would be great," Amber replied enthusiastically. "I never have any problems talking about my career, or myself, for that matter."

Sara was looking forward to spending the evening with Amber. She was never very good with girlfriends. She never had anyone over because she never knew how her mom would react or what her state of mind would be that day. Sara spent most of her time alone reading books or helping her mom get through some crisis or another. She felt haunted at times by the mere thought of spending the rest of her days without any friends. She really wanted to be friends with Amber since her friend list was empty.

Amber began to laugh, bringing Sara back to reality. "By the way, we get treated like crap. But we can talk more when you come up. I'll get things set up, okay? I'm also curious about how things are going with you and Mr. Hunk downstairs."

Sara smiled and said, "He's so sweet, isn't he?"

"You're a lucky girl," Amber said. "I wish I could find someone like that."

Sara replied with a hint of pink in her cheeks, "You give yourself time. You're young and pretty and soon to be a famous movie star. You'll have them knocking down your door."

"I sure hope so," Amber replied. "Single, straight, and good-looking men are a wonderful and rare find in this town."

With that, Amber went up to her apartment, and Sara went to the vacant apartment. The place looked beautiful, and she was so happy with the way the apartment turned out, bright and full of color. Sara remembered everything from cookwear to linen. Her parents would only need the clothes on their backs. She didn't want them to need anything, and they wouldn't. Sara did what she had to do and, as she was leaving, Tom peeked out of his door.

"Hey, what are you doing in there?" he said with a smile.

"Just checking on some last-minute things before my parents arrive," she said, giving him a quick hug. "I want to make sure everything is perfect for them."

"Do you feel like coming in and having something to drink with me?"

"I'm sorry," Sara replied. "I told Amber I would come over for some soup, wine, and a little girl talk. Can I get a rain check?"

"Sure," Tom said, giving Sara a gentle kiss. "I'll see you later, okay?"

"Yea, you bet," Sara replied. Tom went back into his apartment and gave Sara a quick smile. There is that creepy, eerie smile again, Sara thought, but quickly dismissed it because she loved him.

She also loved her parents and was determined to give them a fresh start. It was going to be a fresh start for everyone, she thought, as she headed upstairs toward Amber's apartment. The wonderful smell of the soup was making her hungry.

Amber welcomed her into her brightly lit apartment filled with all kinds of stuff. "See why I need two bedrooms?" Amber laughed. "Hey, I have a wonderful idea! I have so many clothes that I would love to get rid of. What size is your mom?"

"She actually looks your size," replied Sara.

"Do you think she might like some of this stuff?" Amber said, indicating a few of the piles of clothes laying around.

"I'm sure she would."

"After dinner, we'll go through it, okay?"

"Sure, that sound like fun. I might even find some new stuff for me."

Amber laughed. "Come on. Let's eat before it gets cold." The two women sat down to freshly warmed bread and two bowls of steaming hot soup. Two glasses of wine already poured also sat on the table.

"I'm sorry about the messy apartment," Amber said, "but every time I get back from a movie shoot, it takes me two weeks to unpack. Then it's time to go back to a different shoot."

"I totally understand, and I really appreciate your offer to give my mom the clothes," Sara replied. "She never had really nice things so she will be thrilled."

Amber passed Sara the bread and asked, "So what kind of law do you practice?"

"I mainly do corporate stuff," Sara replied. "Contracts for the company, finalizing big business deals, that sort of thing."

"Wow, you must really be smart to be able to do all that."

"No, usually my boss tells me what he wants and I just put it in the contracts, that's all. But I love my job."

Sara ate a spoonful of soup and added, "Amber, this is the best soup I've ever tasted! Where did you get this?" When Amber told her, Sara replied, "When my parents get into town, I'm going to have to take them there."

Just then Amber noticed something in Sara's soup. It looked like a finger with a gold band at the end, but it was black and swollen as if the ring was cutting off circulation. Amber leaned a little closer to get a better look; she thought she was seeing things. Then she saw what appeared to be an eyeball floating around in the soup's already reddish brown broth. She looked up at Sara and saw a partially dismembered finger on her spoon just before Sara put it in her mouth and began chewing.

Amber jumped up and backwards out of her chair, knocking it onto the ground. She began to gag and thought she was going to vomit. Then the smell came, the smell that made her want run into the bathroom. Sara smelled it, too, but decided to ignore it, not wanting to alarm Amber of what she thought might be coming. But one look at Amber's face, and she knew Amber was the third victim of whatever was haunting this apartment building. She just didn't have the nerve or words to say anything.

Instead Sara asked, "What's wrong? Is there something wrong with the soup?"

"I'm not sure. I thought I saw something strange." Amber looked back at the soup; it was normal, just noodles and vegetables, nothing strange or gross. She slowly picked up her chair and sat back down. "I must be more tired than I thought."

Sara began eating her soup again while Amber just sat there, running her spoon through the liquid. She glanced at Sara's soup and saw it turn a bright red color, like blood. A giant cockroach crawled out of the bowl and around the rim. Amber looked up from the soup to Sara. Her face was black and bloated, with stripes of flesh hanging down, dripping with blood. Amber, frozen with fear in her seat, thought she saw Sara tear off a piece of flesh from her face and offer it to her, but Sara was holding out a piece of bread. Amber then noticed a giant bulge in Sara neck. It was moving like it had a pulse and was about to explode.

Suddenly a snake with red glowing eyes slithered out of Sara's mouth, hissed at Amber, and told her in an unsteady voice, "Mind your own business; stay out of mine." The stench from earlier returned, stronger than before. Amber jumped and screamed as she ran for the bathroom where she vomited. That smell of rotting meat or something that had been dead for a long time was overpowering.

Sara followed her to the bathroom and stood by the door. She could hear Amber gagging and vomiting.

"Amber, what's wrong?"

Amber yelled through the door, "I'll be out in just a minute; I think I'm just jet lagged, that's all."

"Are you sure?"

"Yeah, I'll just be a minute. Finish your dinner." Amber was standing in front of the mirror, wiping her face down with a cold rag. She didn't want to go back out there and see that again. What was going on? She was afraid she might be losing her mind. After ten minutes, Amber exited the bathroom. Sara was sitting at the table sipping on her wine. Everything seemed normal.

"Amber, are you sure you're okay?" Sara asked, a concerned look on her face

"Yeah, I'm fine, just a little overtired is all. I'll be okay." Amber looked down at the table. No fingers, bugs, or snakes. She was relieved.

"Amber, do you want me to leave?" Sara asked

"No! Really, I'm fine. I must have eaten something bad, maybe on the airplane. But I think we'll go through the clothes some other time, if that's okay with you?"

"Of course! I wouldn't think of doing it now, not while you're sick."

Amber sat back at the table, gulped down her glass of wine, and began to go through her soup with her spoon. Everything was normal. She couldn't explain what had just happened, and she wasn't sure she wanted to.

"You go and lay on the couch," Sara said. "I'm going to do the dishes. It's the least I can do after you invited me to dinner."

Amber did not protest and fell asleep on the couch in record time. Sara began to fill up the sink with soapy water and was emptying the unwanted soup into the trash when she saw a giant cockroach in her soup bowl. Did Amber see this? She thought. How can I explain to her all the weird things that have been going on lately? Will stuff start happening to her, too?

Sara finished the dishes and cleaned off the table while Amber slept peacefully on the couch. Sara covered her with a blanket and let herself out. As she was leaving, Tom popped his head out of his apartment.

"Care for a cocktail?"

"Sure."

Amber woke up twenty minutes later and headed straight for her boyfriend's house. She didn't want to stay in her apartment alone after what had happened. Amber had the feeling something was really wrong either with the building or with Sara. Either way, she may have to find a new place to live.

A WALK WITH TOM TO THE PINK HOUSE

Sara headed back to her apartment after she and Tom shared a quick cocktail and conversation. She had some things to take care of for work. She also wanted to see if she could find any history on her building that might explain some of the things that were going on. She went into her office and flipped on her computer. While she waited for it to boot up, Sara went into the kitchen and made herself a cup of tea. She then completed her work and began her search.

Three hours later, she had come up with nothing on either her building or the pink house.

Sara put on her jacket and grabbed her flashlight. She decided to take a fast walk down to the pink house and see if she could find a name or address, something that could help her find out why things were happening.

Sara was walking down the hall steps when Tom stuck his head out of his apartment. "Hey you, kind of late for a walk, don't you think?"

"Feel like coming with me?" Sara asked.

Tom asked where she was going as he opened his door to reveal his hard body; he had on only sweatpants.

Sara said, "I'm going down to that pink house. I need to get an address so I can do a computer search and find out more about what's going on here."

"Sara," Tom replied sternly, "you can't go back to that house, especially this late at night. You don't know what's going to happen. Something evil is living in that house, something really bad. I can feel it just by walking past."

"Listen, Tom, I have to go. I have to find out what's going on. Do you want to go with me or not?"

"Give me a minute to put some clothes on, okay?" Tom said as he turned back into his apartment. "Don't leave without me, do you understand?"

"I won't," Sara promised. "I'll wait right here for you."

Sara sat on the steps until Tom emerged fully dressed ten minutes later.

"Are you sure you want to do this?" Tom asked.

"I'm not sure I want to, but I have to," replied Sara.

They left and headed toward the pink house. As they approached the building, it was creepier than Sara remembered, and both Tom and Sara could feel something evil trying to pull them into the house. But they resisted. Sara found the address, and they headed back to the apartment building, walking very fast to get away from the evil pull they both felt. Tom invited Sara in, but she declined. She still had some work to do for her boss, and she was anxious to get started on her computer search of that pink house. He told her he would see her tomorrow and kissed her goodnight.

Sara walked cautiously toward her apartment. No odors, nothing bad, which was a relief. She didn't want to see anything tonight; she'd had enough. Before entering her apartment, she knocked on Amber's door. No answer. She must have gone out or was still sleeping. Hopefully that means she's feeling better, Sara thought.

Sara entered her apartment and headed for the kitchen to put on water for tea before she got to work. The phone rang; it was Tom.

"Are you okay up there?"

"Yeah…why?" Sara replied.

"I just got such a creepy feeling when we were at that house, I just wanted to make sure you were okay."

"Thank you for asking, but there's nothing out of the ordinary up here."

"Okay," Tom said, "but if I hear any screams, I'm coming up there and will break the door down to get to you."

"That's very sweet," she said, filled with love for him at that moment. "Hopefully it won't be necessary, but I appreciate that you're looking out for me."

"My pleasure. Well good night then. I'll see you tomorrow."

Sara hung up the phone, made herself a cup of tea, and sat down at her computer. Sara typed in some information and waited for the screen she wanted. Instead she noticed a shadow. It looked like a man and woman in turn-of-the-century clothing. She knew who these people were. They were just sitting in a living room, a child to the right of the woman. The images disappeared, and Sara thought she was just spooked and scaring herself.

But then the entire screen was filled with the image of a woman's face. Sara just stared at it, wondering what was going to happen next. The face changed. It went from normal looking to blue and bloated, with strips of flesh hanging off. Blood oozed from the cuts on this woman's face. Black holes replaced her eyeballs, and cockroaches and snakes slithered in and out of them.

Sara pushed her chair back, trying to escape the horror that was before her. She felt something crawling up her arm. It was a cockroach. She jumped to her feet, swiping away the bug, but not before it bit her. Sara could smell that distinguishing odor of death and decay and ran for the front room to get away from it, almost falling over Ben who seemed to be in her path at the oddest times.

When Sara reached her front room, she heard a woman's voice utter her name very softly, "SSAARRAA." Chills ran up and down her spine; it was the most eerie sound she had ever heard. Sara quickly opened her patio door, trying to get that smell out of her nostrils and voice out of her ears. She felt like vomiting.

After being outside for twenty minutes and trying to air out that smell from her apartment, she went back in. Cautiously she walked around the apartment, afraid of what she might find. She entered her office and held her breath. Everything was normal. She leaned on the doorframe and began to cry, softly at first and then she let loose, releasing all her emotions. What was going on and will it ever stop? she thought through her tears. Was the answer in the basement? Was it connected to the pink house?

Sara decided to go back into the room in the basement and look for answers. She reached the room, flashlight in hand, and took a deep breath. The door was heavier than she remembered, but she was still able to open it. She found the chain and pulled it down, lighting the tiffany lamps and giving the room a green, eerie glow. Sara wanted to go through more of the books and take that diary upstairs. Maybe she missed something when she read it earlier.

Sara stood on the bookcase to reach the top shelves, but it wasn't very secure so she got down. She was afraid she might fall, and no one would know she was there. She took the flashlight and aimed a beam of light at it, revealing a vertical crack that ran top to bottom. Sara could feel a cool breeze coming through the crack. What was on the other side of that bookcase? She pushed it with all her might and was finally able to move it enough to see there was another room back there. This room had no lights, so she turned on her flashlight and entered carefully.

The moment she entered the room, Sara felt like she had let something evil out that might haunt her more than ever. It felt like when she and Tom were at the pink house, like she was being drawn to something. The odor returned, and it was even stronger than before. Sara felt like vomiting again and running out of this evil placed, but something kept her moving deeper into the room.

She soon found a large metal staircase. Sara aimed the flashlight beam upwards to see what kind of staircase it was

Awakened Dreams

and where it led. It was a spiral staircase, but Sara couldn't see where it stopped; it was too dark. Sara decided to venture upward. The spiral staircase was unsteady and moved with every step she took. She made it all the way to the top where the staircase just ended. Sara aimed the beam of the flashlight and could see a hatch of some kind. She tried to open it, but it wouldn't budge. She knew that directly above was the roof. How interesting, she thought, a secret room that led to a secret staircase that leads to a hatch that goes up to the roof.

There was nothing more she could do, so Sara started to head back down the spiral staircase, holding on for dear life and praying the entire thing wouldn't come crashing down with her on it.

Sara got down safely and went to get Tom. She needed to show him this. He was still up when she knocked on his door.

"Hey," he said, "what's going on?"

"Come on," Sara said. "You have to see what I found. Hurry up, get dressed. Oh, you weren't ready to go to bed, were you?"

Tom looked at his watch; it was 9:30. "No, I was just finishing up some last-minute paperwork. Give me a minute; I'll be right out."

A few minutes later, Tom emerged from his apartment fully dressed and wide awake. "OK, Sara, what's the big find?"

"Come with me, and I'll show you." Sara led Tom downstairs and into the secret room. Then she showed him the bookcase and the newly found secret room and the spiral staircase.

"Wow," Tom exclaimed. "This is weird. Why would they put a staircase here?"

"Go up and try to open the hatch, will you?"

"What hatch?"

"There's a hatch up there," Sara said, pointing upward. "I think it leads to the roof. I can't open it. Will you try?"

"Sara, I don't think this staircase is very safe."

"It's loose, but you'll make it. Just be careful." Sara handed Tom the flashlight and gave him a kiss for luck.

"How did you find this?" he asked as he began to climb.

"I came down here to go through some of those books, and I noticed the shelf was loose so I pushed it out of the way and just sort of opened it."

Tom was halfway to the top. "Sara. if you're ever going to use these stairs. you're going to need to get them fixed."

"I know, and I will. Listen, I'll be right back. Stay up there. I'm going to the roof to see where this opening is and make sure there's nothing else under here. When I pound, you pound, okay?"

"Fine, but hurry up." Tom aimed the flashlight at the hatch Sara was talking about and pushed on it, but he felt like he was pushing the metal staircase down instead of pushing up on the hatch. When the stairway shook, he stopped quickly, grabbed both of the railings, and dropped the flashlight all the way down the staircase. Sara tried to jump out of the way, but it hit her in the leg,

"Ouch," she yelled.

"Sara, did you get hit with the flashlight?" Tom yelled.

"Yeah, but I'm okay. I'm going to the roof now; don't move."

"Just hurry up, will you?" Tom replied.

"Why, you got a hot date or something?" she joked. Tom laughed in return.

"You know, people make all kinds of modifications to these old houses. I wouldn't be surprised if you find more. I wonder if anyone discovered this before you."

"I almost feel like I really was the one meant to find it, like I was drawn to it or something," Sara said. "I know that sounds weird, but it's how I feel."

The room echoed with their voices, making it creepier and eerier than Sara liked. She ran up the stairs and into her apartment, opened her kitchen window, and climbed out onto the roof. She figured out where the hatch was and began to pound. Tom began to pound back.

"Tom, thanks for doing that," Sara said when she returned to the basement. "We'll get a better look tomorrow when it's light out."

"Sara, I think that staircase leads to an old entrance to the roof," Tom said when he was safely on the ground. "People used to have chicken coops and pigeon houses on roofs. Maybe that's what it was used for."

"I thought the same thing," Sara replied. "I would really like to open it, maybe do something with the roof; it would make a nice patio for everyone to enjoy on beautiful nights."

"Tomorrow we'll come down here and check it out more. Right now I have to get to bed. I've got to get up early. I have a business meeting." Tom looked at Sara with his big dark eyes. "I'll see you tomorrow evening when I get home from work. I really wouldn't use the stairs again until someone can come check them out. I have a friend who is an engineer. I'll get him to come out tomorrow and tell us what we need to do to make those stairs secure, OK?"

Sara gave Tom a hug. "You're wonderful, you know that? I'm not going anywhere tomorrow, so just give me a call and let me know if and when he's coming."

Tom left to go back to his apartment, and Sara stayed downstairs to pick up the discarded books. She never did find that diary she set out to find; she forgot all about it.

That night Sara had no nightmares, just a good night sleep after taking a well-needed bubble bath. She awoke at 7:30 feeling alive and refreshed. She got up and made herself some coffee, with toast and jam, and sat in front of the TV and watched the news. Thirty minutes later, she got up and got dressed; she had a lot of things to do. Sara went into her office, completed the documents she needed for work, and faxed them to her secretary who would take care of them.

After completing her work, she tried another search for any information on the pink house, but didn't learn much. She asked her secretary if she could do some research on the address she gave her; she agreed and promised to let Sara know as soon as she found out anything.

At 3:30 Sara was pleasantly surprised to hear Tom coming home earlier than usual. A moment later, she heard a knock at her door.

"I just wanted to let you know my engineer friend will be here in about an hour, okay?"

"Great," replied Sara, happy to see him. "Come on in. Would you like something to drink? Water, tea, or a glass of wine maybe?"

"Yeah, that sounds great." Sara and Tom walked into the kitchen. Tom got the bottle of wine from the refrigerator while Sara fetched two glasses.

"I would really like to get all this stuff sorted out before my parents get here," Sara said. "I don't want them to know what's going on, and I certainly don't want them to see the things we've been seeing. This is going to be a new start, a new life for them. They couldn't handle seeing this stuff."

"I know," Tom replied. "I'm having a hard time myself trying to understand. I can't even close my eyes without seeing something. I'm afraid something bad is going to happen. I just have this feeling, and it's almost consuming me."

Sara put her arms around him and said, "We really need to stick together. Things don't happen as much when we're together. Have you noticed that?"

"Not really. Maybe it's because these are the most horrible images I've ever seen." Tom shuddered and added, "Sara, when are you back to work?"

"In a couple of weeks," she answered. "The nice thing is I can work from home most of the time if I need to; my boss really doesn't care one way or another. I don't think I would be able to concentrate on anything right now so being off is pretty good timing."

They settled on the couch with their glasses of wine and Sara asked, "Tom, I want to know more about you. You're from Ohio, right?"

"Yeah. I'm the fourth of six kids. We grew up on a big farm, about 1,550 acres, and it was really hard work. Two of my brothers still help with the farm. My two older sisters are married with kids of their own, but they all live in the same town. My parents are getting up in age, so everyone pitches in to help. They were mad at me for leaving, but I just didn't see any future in that town or in farming, though I miss it sometimes. My oldest brother lives in Boston; he went to school there on a full athletic scholarship and loved it so much that he stayed. He's the one that encouraged me to leave. I'd probably still be working on the farm with not much of a future without him."

Sara and Tom spent the rest of the day together, getting to know each other and where they came from. Sara was taken by Tom and Tom by her. They were falling in love with each other, all over again. Tom spent the night; Sara loved having him in her bed when she fell asleep and waking up to him in the morning. She felt safe in Tom's arms, loved and wanted, a feeling long forgotten and dearly missed.

THUMP, THUMP

The next morning Sara needed to do some laundry. After Tom left for work, she gathered her things and headed downstairs. She decided to go through more of the books while she waited for her laundry to get done. Sara went through a whole bookshelf during the washing cycle. She put her clothes in the dryer and went back to her work.

While sorting through another shelf of books, Sara heard a sudden and loud THUMP, THUMP, THUMP. She slowly walked over to the dryer where the sound seemed loudest.

Sara closed her eyes, afraid of what she might find, and took a deep breath. When she opened the first dryer door, she screamed and jumped backwards. In the dryer was the severed head of her father. It looked like it had simply been pulled off his body. The edges were ragged and dirty; the face looked bloated, black and blue; the eyes and mouth were wide open and crawling with maggots. Blood was everywhere in the dryer, all over her clothing.

Sara began to scream and clasped her hands over her mouth, trying not to vomit. She could hear the same thumping noise coming from the other dryer and was afraid to look inside; she knew what horrid thing she would find. Sara slowly approached the second dryer, placed her hand on the handle, and could feel the force of whatever was inside shaking the dryer and making that noise. When she opened the dryer, her fears were realized. Inside was the head of her mother.

Sara screamed and ran up the basement stairs straight to her apartment. She called Tom and explained to him, fully hysterical and almost incoherent at times, what she found. She kept asking him, how did they get here, they weren't due to arrive for some time, who would do such a horrible thing to her parents…

Tom couldn't believe what she was telling him; he needed to come home right away and help her. After what seemed to be hours, Tom made it back to the apartment building and went directly up to Sara's apartment where she was hysterically pacing back and forth. Tom wrapped his arms around her and told her everything would be okay.

"Stay here," he said. "I'll go check it out."

Sara refused to be left alone, not even for a minute, so they both headed down to the scene of Sara's horror. Tom peeked into the dryers and found nothing except clothes. No blood, no heads.

"Tom, I don't understand," Sara said in dismay. "I know what I saw. There were two heads, one in each dryer. One was my mother, and the other was my father. Everything in the dryers was covered in blood. I swear it!"

"I believe you, Sara, but everything's gone now," he said gently. Sara began to cry again and ran up the basement stairs back to her apartment.

Tom followed her, saying, "Sara, honey, you have to calm down. Everything's okay."

"No, it's not!" she cried. "I saw my parents' heads in those dryers. I tried calling them, but I can't reach them. What if my parents are really dead and someone is trying to drive me crazy?" The mere vision of her parents decapitated was too much for her. She felt like she wasn't as strong as she once thought. Yes, in front of the man she loved, she was losing her mind.

Later that evening, Sara finally got hold of her mom and was so relieved, she felt like her heart had been placed back into her chest after being ripped out. At the same time, she was confused. Why did she see something like that? What could possibly be going on in her mind that she could literally see something so horrible and out of control as her dead parents' heads? Despite her mom's reassurance that all was well and that her parents would be there in a week or two, Sara felt like she needed to see them. Sara wanted to fly to Chicago and see them for herself; she didn't trust anyone or anything any more. Her mom told her to stop being silly, and she calmed down.

Meanwhile, Tom headed back downstairs. When he reached the basement door, he heard someone say in a low voice, "Next time it might be your head." Tom turned to see who might have said that, but nobody was there. He went downstairs to collect Sara's clothing and found it all on the floor, dirty and in need of rewashing. Tom picked it up and placed them back into the washers, then went back upstairs to Sara's apartment. Sara was sitting on the couch. He walked in and called her name; she didn't respond.

"Sara," Tom yelled. Nothing. He went to the couch and sat beside her, took her by both shoulders, and began to shake her lightly. Sara turned her head and just looked at him. She had a blank stare and empty eyes. Tom was about to shake her harder or perhaps slap her when she finally answered him.

"What?" The only thing that Sara could see was Tom with a bloated, black face with his skin shredded to pieces. She tried to scream, but nothing came out. What Tom saw was her moyth open as wide as it would go and the most horrid look of terror on her face that he had ever seen.

"Sara, are you okay?"

"What," she said, seeming to come back from wherever she was. "Yes, what's going on?"

"You were in your own world."

Sara had such a funny look on her face. She was pale, and drops of sweat were beginning to form on her forehead. Tom went to the bathroom and soaked a washcloth in cold water. When he placed it on her forehead, she instantly felt better. Tom also got her a glass of water, which she drank in one gulp. Sara then lay down on the couch for several hours. Tom stayed to make sure she was okay.

When Sara finally got up, Tom was preparing something to eat. As they sat and enjoyed soup and sandwiches, Tom said, "You look much better than you did earlier."

"I thought I was going out of my head, seeing things that weren't there," she replied. "I think I've been under too much stress."

"How do you feel about going away for the weekend?"

Either he could read her mind or he had talked to her mother, she thought, since her mom had suggested a getaway earlier that day. Sara started to get suspicious. Were the two of them talking about her behind her back? Were they plotting something or was this just a coincidence? Either way she was going to make it work to her advantage. She would have Tom all to herself, and she might even get back some of her sanity in the process. Maybe she could find out what he really was up to.

Sara stated, "I would love that more than anything else. When can we leave?"

"Let me make some arrangements, and maybe we can leave tomorrow."

Sara gave Tom a gentle kiss on the lips, and he gave her the same. They ended up in each other's arms, making love. Sara had never felt so close to anyone in her life. She loved him so much, yet she felt uneasy somehow. Something didn't feel quite right and she couldn't put her finger on it. Maybe the weekend would help her figure it out.

Before Tom left to go back to his apartment and do some paperwork, he asked Sara if she was going to be okay.

"Yes," she reassured him. "But if you hear me scream, I want you to run in here."

"I will," he promised. "I love you, Sara."

"I love you, too," Sara replied.

Tom knocked on Sara's door an hour later. "Hey, great news," he said when Sara opened the door. "I managed to book reservations for the next couple nights at a bed and breakfast about two hours from here. They had a cancellation and were able to take us."

Sara jumped into Tom's arms and gave him a great big kiss. "You are the most wonderful man in the world!"

Tom laughed and said, "How soon can you be ready? I booked it for three days."

"I'm ready; I packed while you were downstairs."

"Good. Me, too," Tom said.

"Then let's go."

"Wait. What about Ben?"

"Let's leave him in the basement; we can put his litter box and enough food for a couple of days down there," Tom suggested.

"I'll call Amber and see if she can check on him from time to time. Matter of fact, let me run over to her place now." Sara went across the hall and knocked on Amber's door. Luckily she was home.

"Hey Amber, can you do Tom and me a favor?"

"Sure, what do you need?"

"We are going out of town for a few days. I'm going to leave Ben in the basement with his litter box and food. Will you check on him?"

"You don't have to do that. I'll take him here until you get back."

"Are you sure?"

"Yeah, I love cats."

"Thank you so much, Amber. I promise I'll make it up to you."

"No problem. When are you leaving?"

"In a few minutes. It's a spur of the moment thing."

"OK, just bring him over here; I'll take care of him." Sara gathered his food, litter box, and some toys. Tom had Ben in his arms. Ben was fighting to get down, but Tom had a good grip on him. After they dropped Ben off with Amber, they left.

THE INN

They drove for two hours, finally reaching the bed and breakfast. They were so looking forward to finally relaxing and being with each other. They checked in and unpacked. The room in which they were staying in was so cute. It was on the first floor and had a view of the woods and its own bathroom. The bed sat on a pedestal high off the floor. The hardwood floor was partially covered by a flowered area rug, and the wallpaper was white with blue and purple flowers. The room was very feminine, but Tom didn't mind. He loved this inn; he was personal friends of the owners, Laura and Mark Chevy, and did work for them.

After a wonderful home-cooked meal, Sara and Tom decided to go for a walk in the woods; they walked hand in hand, just talking, and Sara never felt closer to Tom. After about two hours, they turned around to head back to the inn. The woods looked dark, and they could hear the different animals coming alive.

The noises spooked Sara a little, and she asked Tom, "We aren't lost, are we?"

"No. We just walked straight down the road; it should be pretty easy to find our way back."

"Are you sure we're still on the road?"

"Sara, don't worry," Tom said, squeezing her hand. "We'll get back okay."

Sara and Tom headed back, both with smiles on their faces. Sara held the flashlight up to her face and made funny faces at Tom as they walked, and he did the same. They were laughing and enjoying each other's company.

After an hour and half, Sara turned and looked at Tom. "I don't see anything yet, no lights or anything."

"Don't worry," Tom said. "We are still a little ways away. We should be coming up to the inn soon."

"Okay. I just don't want to get lost out here, that's all." As they were walking, Sara could swear she heard footsteps behind her. She stopped to listen.

"Tom," Sara whispered, "do you hear someone or something behind us?"

"No," he answered lightly. "I don't hear anything except animals running around in the woods, which is what they do."

"I swear there's someone behind us, following us," she said.

Tom stopped and turned to Sara. "I think it's just your imagination. You're so spooked about everything that's been going on, you're starting to hear things."

"Yeah, maybe you're right. I think I need to just stay in bed for a couple of days. Would you like to join me?" she asked suggestively.

"I would love to," Tom replied. "That's why we're here, to enjoy each other and get away for a while."

Just then, Tom heard the bushes move behind him. Sara heard it, too, and they both turned at the same time.

"Did you hear that?" Sara asked.

"Yeah, that time I did," Tom answered.

"We are definitely not alone anymore," Sara stated.

"I'm telling you, it's just some animal. Most forest animals are nocturnal; they like the darkness. Listen for a minute."

Tom and Sara stood quietly looking around trying to find out the source of the noise. Aiming the flashlight into the bushes, Tom saw it first, then Sara. A large man emerged from the brush and just stood there, doing and saying nothing.

Tom yelled to him, "Hey, are we close to the Mountain View Inn?" The man didn't say a word; he didn't move. He continued to just stand there.

Sara looked at Tom. "I get the feeling he's not friendly. Let's get out of here." They turned and began to walk quickly down the road. Both were relieved when they finally saw the lights of the inn. They went up to their room, took a shower together, lay in bed, and just held each other.

Sara got up to use the bathroom and hit her big toe on the corner of the dresser. She yelped in pain and grabbed her big toe. When she made it to the bathroom, she sat on the toilet and looked at her injured toe. Sara heard something moving in the room; she thought it was Tom getting up to see what the yelling was about. But when she headed back to the bed, Tom was fast asleep. She looked around somewhat confused; she could have sworn she heard someone moving around in the room.

When she crawled back into bed, Tom turned and put his arms around her. Just as she began to fall back to sleep, she heard and the noise again. Someone was in the room. She sat straight up in the bed and began looking around. She couldn't see anyone, but she could hear footsteps. She looked over and saw the shadow of a large figure standing in the window. She screamed as loud as she could.

Tom bolted up, "What! What!"

"Someone's in the window!"

Tom jumped up, put on his robe, and ran outside. Sara followed. Standing there was Mark Chevy. He was a pretty big man, and he was drunk.

His wife Laura came running out. "What's going on," she yelled.

"There was somebody in our window."

"It was just me," Mark said. "I couldn't get in. I left my keys on the table."

Sara was relieved it wasn't just the owner; she had been so jumpy lately with everything going on. Laura was yelling at him, telling him he scared everybody to death. Both Mark and Laura apologized to Sara and Tom for the scare.

Once back in their room, Sara just sat in the chair. Her heart was racing, and her adrenaline was flowing; she wasn't going back to sleep anytime soon. Tom lay back down and fell instantly asleep. The next thing Sara knew, the sun was shining in her face, waking her up. She looked at the clock—it was 7:30. Tom was gone; he must have gotten up early. Sara took a shower, got dressed, and went into the kitchen. She could smell fresh coffee brewing and guests laughing and talking.

Tom was sitting at a table. He greeted her with a hug and a smile. "Hey, sleepyhead, you finally got up. Want a cup of coffee?"

"That sounds wonderful," she replied.

Tom got up and poured Sara a cup of coffee. "Feel like a walk after breakfast?" he asked as he sat back down.

They decided to walk into town and browse through the antique stores. Sara wanted to see if she could find something nice for Amber and her parents. After a couple hours of looking and not finding anything, Sara and Tom headed back to the inn and took a nap before lunch. Sara hadn't been this relaxed in weeks.

Later that night, they were sitting in the living room, enjoying the crackling fire in the big stone fireplace, when Sara heard thunder, and it began to rain. A bad storm was moving in. Laura asked Mark to go check the generator just in case the electricity went out. Tom went with him. "Things get pretty wild around here with some of the storms we get," she said. "The weather report said this might be a good one."

The weather report was right. The thunder came faster and louder, and the lighting was almost blinding at times. Sara was a little scared. Tom and Mark hadn't come back yet. She waited anxiously by the window and was relieved whenTom came in, though he seemed worried about something.

"Where's Mark?" Laura asked as she entered the room.

"I don't know," Tom responded, sounding concerned. "He was right behind me a minute ago and then he just disappeared. I think I saw him head toward that little shack you have out back."

"That's just an old well house; there is nothing out there," Laura said, looking out the kitchen window. "Hey, there's somebody out there!"

"Who?" Tom asked, joining her at the window. She saw a large figure just standing there in the rain.

"That's got to be Mark. What is he doing just standing there getting soaked?"

Tom grabbed a flashlight. "I'll go see what he's doing. Maybe he needs help with something. I'm not sure he knows I came back in."

Sara looked at Tom and said in a worried voice, "Please be careful. I don't want you to get struck by lighting or anything."

"Don't worry," he said, kissing her on the forehead. Tom put on a rain poncho, grabbed a flashlight, and left through the back door. Sara could see him heading toward the figure, but then she lost sight of him; the rain was coming down too hard.

Tom headed for the old well house; the figure was still there. Tom couldn't see his face, but he noticed something in his hand. When he got almost face to face with the figure, he realized it was Mark, and he had an axe in his hand.

Tom stopped dead in his tracks. Mark raised the axe and tried to strike Tom with it, but the younger and faster Tom was able to move out of the way before it came down. He slid in the mud but quickly got up and ran toward the woods, dropping his flashlight in the process.

From their vantage point, Laura, Sara, and several of the other guests couldn't quite make out what was going on, but they could see the shadows and beams of the flashlights going everywhere. Sara ran out the front door and began to scream for Tom. When he didn't answer, Sara began to put on a raincoat, but Laura stopped her.

"Laura, I have to go and see about Tom," Sara pleaded. "He could be out there hurt; he may need some help."

Laura looked at Sara. "If you go out there you may be the next person who needs help. Tom can take care of himself.

You stay here with us. I mean it; don't go out there. Tom will be back; we need to protect ourselves right now until we find out what's really going on."

Laura looked out the window and saw a large figure approaching the inn with an axe in his hand. She ran for the front door and locked it. Sara ran to lock the back door and all the windows. When she ran back to the kitchen window, the large shadow was gone.

"Where did he go?" Sara yelled. "Where's Tom!"

Laura didn't know. She didn't even know where Mark was. She opened the back door and began to yell for Mark. Sara yelled at her to close the door, but Laura ran outside instead. She wanted to find Mark and find out if he was the one who tried to attack Tom with the axe. She soon disappeared in the heavy rain and fog that was beginning to roll in, making the beams of light from the house look like ghostly images dancing around.

Sara was yelling for Laura to come back, but nothing. No Laura, Mark, or Tom. Sara feared the worst and was terrified. She shut the door and quickly turned when she heard someone down in the basement. Someone had gotten in through the bulkhead door. Sara took the poker from the fireplace and ran it through the S-shaped handles of the door that led down to the basement from the kitchen.

Suddenly Sara could hear Laura screaming. Pam and Steve, another couple staying at the inn, burst into the kitchen. "Where are Tom and Mark? What the hell is going on?" Steve demanded. Pam was a nurse, and Steve was an accountant. Neither of them knew what was going on, and they didn't care. They just wanted all this to end; they wanted everyone to come back into the house and wait out the storm.

Sara was standing by the kitchen door, not knowing what to say to Steve, when she heard someone bang at the front door. She ran as fast as she could, hoping it was Tom. But when she moved the curtains away, she saw it was Mark. He looked different. His eyes were empty, and he had a half smile on his face which scared her to death.

"Sara," Mark said slowly, "let me in. I want to show you something."

"No!" Sara yelled. Just then Mark raised his hand. He was holding Laura's head by the hair. Her eyes were wide open, and her mouth looked like it was about to scream. But Sara screamed instead, in horror..

"Come on, Sara, let me in," Mark persisted. "I promise I won't hurt you. Tom's out here. He's wet; he wants to come in and get out of the rain."

Sara turned away from the door, sank to the floor, and began to cry. Mark began to bang on the door with his fists. Then Sara heard a crack. The axe came through the wooden door, missing her head by inches. She got up and ran into the kitchen where Pam and Steve were still standing.

"Who the hell is that?" Pam asked with fear in her voice.

"It's Mark," Sara cried. "He killed Laura—he cut her head off, and he has it with him. We have to make a run for it. Steve, do you have your car keys handy?"

"Yeah, they're right here."

"We need to try and run for the car. We need to get out of here before we end up like Laura."

"Oh my God," Pam screamed. "What if we just hide? Maybe he wouldn't be able to find us."

"He knows this house like the back of his hand; we got to get out of here. NOW! Mark's in front, and the cars are parked out back. Mark, do you think you could sneak out, unlock your car, and get ready to take off fast when you see us coming?"

Both Pam and Steve nodded, and Steve went out the back way. A minute later, Sara and Pam made a run for it, just as Mark came around to the back of the house. Sara yelled for Steve to start the car. They piled in and locked the doors as Steve put the car in reverse, swung the car around, and hit the gas just as Mark reached for the car door. They tore off down the tree-lined road.

All of a sudden, Steve saw someone in the middle of the road. It was Tom. Steve swerved, barely missing Tom, and ended up crashing head-on into a tree. Sara hit her head on the side window, shattering it; she was dazed and losing consciousness. Steve's air bag deployed so he was not injured. Pam was not so lucky. A tree branch had come right through the window, impaling her in the chest. She was dead.

Steve just sat there, screaming for Pam to wake up. Sara was trying to focus. She saw Tom coming toward her. He opened the door, picked her up, and sat her down on the grass. She was fighting to remain conscious.

"Sara, Sara? Are you okay?" Tom pleaded.

She was holding the right side of her head. "Yeah, just give me a minute." The rain was coming down even harder, which was good for Sara; it kept her from going completely out.

Tom got Sara to her feet and stuck his head into the driver's-side window. "Steve, we have to get out of here."

"I don't want to leave her."

"Steve, we can't help her now. We have to go!" Tom tried to open Steve's car door but it wouldn't budge. "You'll have to climb over the seat and get out through the back door."

Steve did as he was told and was getting out of the car when Mark appeared. Sara began to scream, and Tom ran toward Mark, trying to get the axe out of his hand. Mark pushed Tom out of the way and brought the axe down and into Steve's back.

Sara and Tom started to run toward town, a mile or so away. Sara's head was pounding, and Tom was holding her up as they ran. Tom looked back and could see the axe coming up and going down, over and over. He knew what Mark was doing—cutting Steve into many pieces.

Sara and Tom made it into town and found the small police station, but the doors were locked. They started banging on the door, and someone finally came. When the door opened, Sara and Tom ran inside, closing and locking the door behind them.

"What's going on?" the policeman demanded.

"There is a crazy man out there," Tom said. "He's already killed several people, and now he's after us."

Sara and Tom gave the officer the full details of what happened, and he got on the radio and called for backup. Sergeant Lou Briggs was in charge of the investigation. He called an ambulance for Sara—she had a nasty cut on her head—and Tom went with her to the hospital. In the morning after Sara was released, the police drove them back to the inn. They went past where the car had crashed into the tree; it was cordoned off with yellow police tape. The house and part of the road were cordoned off as well.

After exiting the police car, Sara and Tom slowly walked up to the front door of the inn, which was covered with axe marks. Sara went directly to the room in which they stayed. It was a shambles. All of the clothes were ripped into shreds;

the mattress was torn and its insides were strewn everywhere. Sara turned to Tom and said, "Let's just go. We'll leave everything. Let's just go home."

Sara's getaway was a nightmare worse than the one she tried to escape from. The police said Laura's head was found on the front porch; the rest of her body has not been recovered. Steve and Pam were found by their car, and another couple staying in the inn was found hacked up and hanging behind the old well house. As far as the police knew, Mark, had done all this. They speculated he had some kind of mental illness history and had stopped taking his medication. He allegedly went crazy and killed everyone, except Sara and Tom.

Sara tried to find her purse, but it had disappeared. "Tom, I think he took my purse," she cried. "My license with my address was in there. Tom, he knows where I live!"

"Oh, my God," Tom replied. "We will need some protection until Mark is caught." Tom spoke with the local police, who took them. The police went in first; they checked the basement and all areas of the apartment building. There was no sign of Mark anywhere. The police thought he was long gone but set up twenty-four-hour surveillance around Sara's building just in case.

Several days later, the police notified Sara and Tom that they had found Mark hanging from a tree not far from where the car accident occurred. They said he had been there several days. Sara cried at the news. She was sad the whole thing happened and relieved he was found. Now maybe they could sleep at least a little easier at night.

THE CRASH

Two quiet weeks had passed since her nightmare had ended, and Sara sat on the couch with a cup of tea. Today was the day she was going to pick up her parents from the airport. Her parents were coming in on Flight 298, due to arrive at 4:30 p.m., in the heart of rush hour traffic. Tom was getting off early to go with her to greet her parents. She was very excited to see them, but she was also worried. In his last letter, her dad said her mom wasn't doing so well, and he was afraid she might end up in the hospital again. Sara didn't want that to happen so close to their move or after they arrived. She wanted everything to be perfect.

Sara sat in front of the TV and was absentmindedly watching a game show when a special news brief came on; it was about a plane crash that had just occurred in Chicago. The newscaster, who Sara had seen somewhere before but couldn't put her finger on it, said Flight 298, Chicago to California, had crashed somewhere in rural Illinois twenty minutes into flight. Her parents' flight.

Sara dropped her cup of tea and just sat there in shock. She raised her hand to cover her mouth and muffle the screams trying to escape her mouth. Tears began to roll down her cheeks as overwhelming sadness filled her. She could feel it rising from her feet up to her head. Pain hit her in the pit of her stomach. How could this be? she thought. It had to be a dream. Everything had to be a dream.

On the end table was a piece of paper with Sara's parents' flight information written on it. Sara picked it up and prayed it didn't say Flight 298. But it did—Flight 298 leaving Chicago at 8:45 a.m. and arriving in California at 4:30 p.m.

Sara didn't know what to do next, who to call, where to go. She was totally confused as to exactly what was going on and what she had to do to find out. She headed into the bedroom. The first thing she needed to do was get dressed; she did know that much.

Several minutes later, the news commentator came on with another update, and it wasn't good: The rescue workers claimed all the passengers apparently perished in the crash. Sara's tears began to flow anew. No! Not my parents. She dialed Tom's cell number, and he answered almost immediately. Sara was now crying so hysterically, Tom could barely make out one word she was saying. Finally she calmed down enough to tell Tom what she had heard on the news.

"I'll be right home, and I'll take you to the airport, okay?" he said in a soothing voice. "Just hold on and don't go anywhere."

When Tom pulled up in from of the apartment building 10 minutes later, Sara was eagerly waiting outside for him. He could see her eyes were red and swollen from crying, and all he wanted to do was comfort her.

As soon as the car stopped, Sara hopped in and said, "We have to get to the airport."

"What's going on?" Tom asked as he pulled away from the curb. "I didn't understand everything you said on the phone."

"My parents' plane crashed, and they are dead," Sara said, beginning to cry again. "I really need to talk to someone at the airport and find out what really happened."

"Okay," Tom said. The airport was about forty minutes away; they made it in twenty. Tom let Sara off at the front entrance while he parked the truck.

Sara ran toward Gate 11 where the plane would have arrived. She ran as fast as she could, not noticing much of anything except the many travelers. Sara also noticed there were no reporters and no hordes of family members demanding information on their loved ones. Something wasn't right, but she couldn't quite put her finger on it.

Sara went directly to the desk at Gate 11 and asked the young girl about any plane crashes. She looked to be about 25, and her name tag said "Hello, my name is Tammy." She looked at Sara with the strangest look. Sara repeated her question, "Where do I go to find out about the plane crash that happened in Chicago?"

"I'm sorry, Miss," Tammy replied. "I don't know what you're talking about." Sara told the girl she heard a special report on the news about Flight 298 crashing in rural Illinois that morning. Tammy got on the phone and called her supervisor. A tall blonde woman came immediately out from behind a closed door and walked over to Sara.

"Hi, I'm Nina Gills, the supervisor," she said as she shook Sara's hand. "How can I help you today?" Sara repeated what she had told Tammy, who was on the phone with Security. When she hung up, she walked over to where Sara and Nina were standing.

"I'm not sure what you saw on TV, but that flight is in the air and due to arrive on time," she said. Sara just looked at both women with amazement. She didn't know if they were trying to hide what was going on or if she was just losing her mind.

"What the hell are you trying to hide?" Sara screamed. "There was a plane crash; I heard it on the news!"

"Please keep your voice down!" Nina demanded. "You are scaring the other passengers ready to board their flights. I'll have to get security here if you don't calm down."

Just then Tom walked up and asked Sara, "What's going on? Did you find out about the crash?"

Sara just looked at Tom and said, "There was no plane crash." Sara collapsed into Tom's arms, and he slowly walked her over to the nearest fast food stand and got her a drink of water. Nina was right behind them.

"I'm sorry if someone told you there was a plane crash," she said gently. "That's a pretty mean trick to play on someone." Nina asked Tom if he would like to take Sara into a quiet room and let her lie down for a while.

Sara looked at Nina and said, "No, thank you, I'm fine now. I just needed to get a drink of water, that's all. I'll be okay; I just need to see my parents." Sara was fighting the emotion that was beginning to overwhelm her again.

"Well, that flight should be landing at around 4:15 or so," Nina said. "Please feel free to use the quiet room. Just ask Tammy to let you in."

After Sara thanked her, Nina walked over to Tammy and instructed her to let Sara into the quiet room if she wanted to lie down.

"What is wrong with that woman?" Tammy asked.

"I don't know, but she needs some help, that's for sure. Or whoever told her there was a plane crash needs to go to jail. I personally think she is just crazy. I thought I was going to have to call the white coats out on her."

"But she said she saw a special report on TV. How could that be?"

"I honestly don't know," Nina replied. "Let me know when they leave, will you?"

"Sure," Tammy replied.

Meanwhile, Tom was sitting at a table with Sara, who was still trying to figure out what had happened. When he offered to get her a cold drink, Sara said she needed a good stiff drink.

"I'm not sure that's such a good idea, Sara," Tom replied.

"Just one, please. I need a glass of wine or something to calm my nerves."

Tom ordered both of them a glass of white wine and also managed to convince Sara to eat something. He was almost afraid to ask her what really happened. She was walking a tightrope these days with all the things that were happening to her. Tom decided if she wanted to explain what happened, she would, and he was right. After she told him what she saw on TV that morning, she kept apologizing to Tom for pulling him away from his job.

"Don't worry about it," Tom replied. "It was a quiet day, and I'd planned to leave early anyway to come pick up your parents. We just got here a little early, that's all." Tom took Sara's hand. "I really hate to see you so upset and crying with worry."

"I'm okay, really," Sara said with a weak smile. "I just don't know what I saw on that television screen. It was so real, I truly thought my parents were killed in a plane crash. Tom, why would I hear something like that? I don't get it."

Sara couldn't get the whys or hows out of her head. She knew it was the work of whatever was happening in her apartment building, all the crazy things she had been seeing, hearing, and smelling. All the terrifying dreams she'd been having. Sara wasn't sure of anything anymore. Could she rely on any of her senses or was everything make-believe? What if she saw another terrible thing on TV? Should she believe it?

Whatever it was, it knew how to get inside her soul, her head, and now her heart. This frightened Sara more than anything else. She needed to know how to stop it, to make it go away, never to come back and make her feel like she was going crazy and certainly never to make her cry.

Tom and Sara sat at that table for several hours waiting for her parents' flight to arrive. At 4:00 they went and waited by the gate. Sara needed to be right there when they arrived. To Sara's surprise, the flight arrived early, and her parents were among the first passengers off the plane. Mom looks tired, Sara thought. She took a deep breath and decided she needed to be strong—for herself and for her parents.

After hugging each of her parents as hard as she could, Sara introduced them to Tom who told her dad he couldn't wait to sit and talk to him about construction stuff. They gathered Bill and Ann's luggage and headed for the front entrance.

"Tom, I think we need to get a cab for my parents," Sara said. "There won't be enough room in your truck for everyone."

"Okay, but let's put the suitcases in the truck bed so they don't have to worry about that at least."

Sara hailed a cab and gave the driver her address. She and Tom sat quietly in the truck for the 40-minute ride back. They reunited in front of the apartment building, and Sara finally felt better. Her parents were with her, and they were a family again.

"Sara, this place is beautiful," Ann exclaimed when they went inside. "I love the building, and the weather seems perfect."

Sara looked up and noticed the sky was turning gray. She said, "It looks like a storm is brewing. You'll find storms come out of nowhere around here."

"Can't be any worse than Chicago," her dad replied with a chuckle.

"Oh, yes it can!" Sara said.

"We can deal with a little rain," Ann replied. "I love when it rains. Everything smells so fresh and new."

They made it into the building with the entire load of luggage. Sara unlocked the door that led to her parents' new home. When they walked in, her mother was in total awe. She loved the colors and the furniture, and she began to cry.

"Mom, what's wrong?" Sara said. "Don't you like the place?"

"I love it," she replied, giving Sara a big hug. "I just can't believe that I'm going to be living in such a beautiful place, that's all."

"Mom, you won't need anything. I even got you linen and towels, Oh, I forgot to tell you! Amber upstairs has some beautiful clothes she wants to give you. Most of them still have the price tags on them. She didn't want to throw them out and asked if you could use anything. I told her I would ask you. I wasn't sure how you felt about taking things from someone you didn't know."

"Honey," Ann replied softly, "most of my things are second hand from the thrift store."

Sara looked at her mom and said, "Well, you have bought your last hand-me-downs, okay? From now on it's nice new things for your nice new life."

Sara showed her mom around the apartment, and she loved everything. Next she showed her parents the basement and the laundry facilities. Sara noticed something was wrong when her mother stepped into the basement; she had a funny, almost scared look on her face. Once they were back in the apartment, Sara's mom changed into the happy, smiling woman she was when she first stepped into the building. She kept saying how nice everything was, as if she had never lived with such nice things, and Sara realized and remembered she hadn't.

"Mom," Sara said, "if I forgot anything, let me know and we'll go shopping for it. Why don't you make a list and keep track of all the things you need, okay?"

"Sara, I can't think of one thing you left out. Can I ask you a question, though?"

"Sure, Mom," Sara replied. "What is it?"

"When we were in the basement, what was that terrible smell? It smelled really bad, like someone had died down there."

Sara just turned and looked at her mom with a surprised look. "Mom, I don't know what you're talking about. I didn't smell anything."

"Sara, I swear I smelled something. Did you recently have some pipes or water back up or something?"

"I don't think so," Sara replied. "I guess maybe some pipes could have backed up; we have had a lot of rain lately."

Sara tried to ignore what her mom had just said; she didn't want to talk or think about anything that was happening in the apartment building. She began to walk toward the front door.

"I'm going to let you get settled. At eight we'll go get dinner, okay, so be ready. I love you both."

Sara just stood there looking at her parents and loving them deeply. She knew her mom felt something was terribly wrong; her mom had always had a sixth sense about those things. Sara went over and kissed both of them on the cheeks.

"Mom, I really just want you and Dad to get a new fresh start in a new place. I hope everything is what you expected."

"Everything is wonderful," Ann replied, but she still had that concerned look in her eyes.

"See you in a little while," Sara said and headed upstairs toward her apartment. When she reached the top of the staircase, she noticed that offensive odor, and it got stronger with every step she took toward her front door. She entered her apartment with caution, hoping there were no surprises in store for her. The whoile plane crash episode was enough drama for one day. She was just glad her parents were alive and here, and that what she had seen on TV was nothing more than a fictional and temporary loss of her sanity. At least that's what she figured.

Sara felt drained; all her energy was gone. She really needed to take a nap before she and her parents went out to dinner. She laid down on the couch and fell asleep. She was awakened by a light knock at her door. Sara looked up and noticed the room was dark. She yelled she would be right there, switched on the light, and looked down at her watch. It was 8:00. Crap! She jumped up and ran toward the front door. It was Tom.

"Come on, sleepyhead," he smiled and ruffled her tousled hair. "It's time to wake up; your parents are waiting downstairs."

"Just give me a minute," she yawned. "I need to wash my face and wake up." Sara walked into the bathroom and splashed water on her face, then brushed her teeth. Ten minutes later, Tom, Sara, and her parents were in a cab heading for a nice little family restaurant where they enjoyed a lovely dinner.

During the meal, Sara's parents admitted they wished they could have given her a better life and provided for her the way they felt they should have. She told them she knew they did the best they could and that they were together now. Nothing else mattered, and everyone's lives were going to keep getting better from now on. Tom offered Bill a wonderful job which he could begin as soon as he got settled. Tom was very grateful to have such an experienced man starting for him, and Bill was grateful for the opportunity.

Tom told Sara's parents about the first time he saw Sara and how he fell in love with her on sight. Sara just smiled and blushed. She slapped Tom on the shoulder and told him to stop embarrassing her, but inside she felt wonderful.

Tom asked Bill, "So how did you meet Ann?"

"Well," Bill said, "we actually met on a blind date, although we were with different people. I was with this horrible girl, and Ann didn't look like she was enjoying herself either. Our dates knew each other and decided we should meet, so they introduced us. And I heard they married each other a couple of years later."

Bill reached over and gave Ann a gentle kiss on her cheek. She just smiled and looked down as if she was embarrassed "We've been together ever since. I have loved this women since the first time I laid eyes on her. I hope you and Tom are as happy as me and your mother, Sara. If you are, you'll have a wonderful life. You know, we all have our ups and downs. But as long as you keep communicating and are understanding of each other's needs and wants, you can make it. So tell us about your parents, Tom. Are they still together?"

"Yep," Tom replied, "still running the farm with help from my brothers and sisters. They've been together for some time now. They were high school sweethearts. Where

I'm from, everyone knows everyone else, and everyone who isn't related usually gets married. I needed to leave the country life, so I came here to California, got a job at a local construction company, and saved my money until I could buy my own equipment and start my own company. I make good money and have thought about buying my own home, but decided that if I met someone and decided to get married, my future wife would help pick out the house. I do want to get married someday and begin a family, but Sara and I will wait a while."

Sara just turned and looked at Tom in shock. Was he saying he wanted to marry her? Was this the way he was going to ask her, or was he being a gentleman and slightly old-fashioned? Did he want to see her parents' reaction first?

Sara's parents appeared happy for their daughter. They were smiling from ear to ear, and so was Sara, when they left the restaurant. Everyone was tired from the day's events as they got into a cab and drove back to the apartment building; Everyone said their goodnights. Tom asked Sara if she wanted some company, but she declined. She was simply too exhausted after the day's events, but she asked for a rain check. He agreed and kissed her before heading to his apartment.

Sara headed upstairs to her own. No odors or anything out of the ordinary greeted her. She needed a shower, and then she needed her bed. She closed her door and turned to see a white shadow come toward her. It was Ben. She had forgotten to feed him, so she picked him up, headed toward the kitchen, and gently placed him on the counter. He purred while she opened a can of cat food and placed its contents in his new bowl. Ben was meowing and rubbing her while purring. She was glad she had found him sometimes. He was good company.

As he ate, Sara went into her bedroom, got her pajamas and a towel, and headed for the bathroom. She stood outside the door, almost afraid to go inside, afraid of what she might see. She slowly turned the doorknob and tried to smell if anything was out of sorts, but there were no odors. She reached around to flip on the light and opened the door all the way. Everything looked normal, and Sara felt a sense of relief.

She took off her clothes and began to fill the bathtub with hot water, but decided a shower would be quicker. All she wanted was her bed and sleep, but first she wanted a cup of tea. After her shower, Sara headed into the kitchen to put on a pot of water. Something wasn't right. She couldn't put her finger on it, but she knew.

AN EXTRA ITEM

After looking around, she finally realized what was wrong. There was an extra item in her kitchen. A very old and rusted coffee pot was sitting on the stove like a giant tower, right in front of her face. She couldn't figure out how she had missed it earlier, but she did. It reminded Sara of the old coffee pots she had seen in old western movies, made of steel with little specks of white as if someone had spattered paint on it, only this one was the biggest coffee pot she had ever seen. She could imagine it taking two hands to lift when it was full of coffee.

As Sara walked closer to the coffee pot, that awful odor hit her, burning the hair in her nostrils and making her eyes water. The pot was lukewarm. She was afraid to lift the lid. She tried to move it; it was filled with some unknown substance. Sara lifted the coffee pot, walked over to the sink, and tried to pour out its contents. The odor was so bad, she had to place one hand over her nose and mouth to keep from vomiting.

When the contents hit the sink, Sara dropped the coffee pot in the sink and jumped back. Whatever was in the pot was thick and dark brown. Sara turned on another light and took a closer look. It was blood, old blood, and it smelled really bad. Sara turned on the water to wash it away, and the smell became less offensive, which eased her mind.

Sara went to lift the coffee pot out of the sink, and it still felt heavy, as if something was on the bottom of the pot and couldn't fit through the pour spout. Sara looked inside but couldn't see anything; the bottom looked like a dark pit. She decided to try and empty the contents into the garbage disposal so if anything came out that she really didn't want to see, she could easily get rid of it.

She turned over the coffee pot and *plop*! She looked down but couldn't quite make out what the substance was. It was red with black areas, and the smell was truly putrid. Sara reached into her utensil drawer and retrieved a fork. She flipped over the mass and, to her horror, realized it was flesh. She could make out the tiny little pores in the skin, but what really gave it away was a tattoo of the name "Betty" in black block letters.

Sara poked around a little bit and noticed something round, of color, but she couldn't make out what it was because it was covered in blood. She rinsed it off with her hose from the sink and screamed when she realized exactly what it was: an eyeball, pale blue with the nerves still attached, starring straight at her. Sara quickly flipped on the disposal and began to push the flesh into it. She could hear the metal blades tearing into the flesh. Then it sounded much louder as if it hit something hard, like a bone.

Sara ran into the bathroom and threw up her dinner. When she returned to the kitchen, the disposal was only making a slight humming noise so she knew it had done its job. She turned it off and went back into the bathroom to get ready for bed. She washed her face and brushed her teeth, which made her feel much better. But when she looked up and into the mirror, blood was all over her face. She began to scream and could see blood tinging her teeth as well.

Fifteen minutes later, Sara awakened on the bathroom floor, unsure of what happened. As she slowly got up, she noticed her nightgown was wet; she had urinated on herself in her few minutes of unconsciousness. She quickly undressed, took a shower, put on fresh clothing, and headed into the kitchen hoping no horrors would greet her. To her immense relief, there was nothing anywhere, just old coffee grounds in the sink. The pot itself was gone.

Sara just stood there, numb. She didn't know what to think anymore. Were all of these strange happenings real, or was she losing her mind? How does an old coffee pot just disappear into thin air or, for that matter, appear out of thin air? All Sara wanted to do was run away, but she also loved her home and now her parents were here. But she was afraid things might happen to her parents, and she couldn't bear that.

Sara just wanted to scream as loud as she could, for as long as she could. She had always been a rational person who believed things could be explained. But everything that had been happening to her lately defied explanation. She figured someone must be trying to tell her something. Maybe she wasn't listening hard enough.

Sara fell into bed, completely exhausted from the day's events. She was asleep almost immediately, but was soon awakened by something at the foot of her bed, under her blankets, moving quickly from side to side. She thought it was Ben, but it felt smaller than a cat somehow. Sara kicked the blankets off her, jumped out of bed, and reached for the light. The blankets looked normal. She pulled the blankets completely off the bed, and there was nothing there.

She remade her bed and climbed back in. She felt too tired to care; as long as whatever it was was gone, she could drift off to sleep. It must have been Ben, Sara reasoned. He sometimes crawled under the blankets and played with her feet when she tried to sleep.

Sara fell into a deep sleep, and a few minutes later, her first nightmare of the night began. She was walking down a flight of steps wearing a white cotton nightgown with a high neckline, puffy sleeves, and a wide single ruffle running down the front and around the bottom. The stairway was dark, and she didn't have anything in her hands to help her see. She felt blind in the darkness. She descended into a room with cold stone floors. She felt like she could possibly be in the depths of hell. It looked a little like her basement, but it was completely empty.

She kept walking and discovered another set of stairs covered in what appeared to be dirt and rocks that hurt her feet as she walked over them. The stairs led to another room, one that wasdusty, dark, and really unfamiliar to her. The entire floor was covered with the sharp rocks, and she could feel her feet being cut up with every step, but she was being pushed or driven somehow to keep going.

Just as she was approaching another stairway, Sara was awakened by Ben clawing at her feet. She placed Ben on the bedroom floor and told him to go away, but he jumped back up onto the bed and lay next to her torso, swiping at her moving fingers. He finally fell asleep as Sara scratched him behind the ears.

Sara fell asleep, too, and soon found herself at the top of a dark and very scary stairway. Sara started to step onto the first step but tripped and fell down the stairs, hitting her head and passing out.

When Sara finally came around, something with little red eyes was staring at her. It was so close to her face, she had to focus hard to see it. She felt a sudden and severe pain on her left cheek. Something was biting her. No, many of something were biting her hands, legs, and face, and she couldn't move or see what it was in the dark. She could feel warm liquid running down her hands and legs. Was she bleeding? Then something lunged at her, catching her above her right eye. Blood started dripping into her eye, and she couldn't see anything but red. She tried to scream, but something jumped into her mouth to silence her.

Sara sat straight up in her bed. She was covered in sweat, and she hurt all over. She also had a terrible headache. It took her a minute to realize where she was, that it had all been a bad dream.

She laid back down, and when she woke up again, the sky was a brilliant blue with white puffy clouds softly passing by. Sara was standing in a field in that same white nightgown, staring up at the clouds. She looked down, and her arms were covered in blood. They looked like they had been torn to shreds. She raised her nightgown to reveal the same types of wounds on her legs. A single drop of blood fell from her forehead as she was looking down at her legs. She raised her hand to her forehead and wiped away more blood. Only this time, small pieces of flesh accompanied it. She began to scream.

A moment later, she heard knocking on her front door. It was Tom. He had heard her screaming and came running upstairs. "Sara, are you okay? Sara, answer me!"

Sara put on her robe so Tom couldn't see her wounds and ran to the front door. But she only opened it as far as the safety chain would allow.

"Sara," Tom asked in a worried voice, "are you all right? Can I come in?"

"I'm fine. I just had a nightmare, that's all. Go back to bed. Thanks for worrying about me, but I'm okay."

Sara could feel the warmth of the blood trickling down her arms and onto the back of her hands. She hoped Tom would leave before he noticed anything was wrong. She forgot about the marks on her face.

"Sara, what happened?" Tom asked in alarm. Something was clearly not right.

"I was just playing with Ben too hard, and he got a bit carried away. I'm fine," Sara said as lightly as she could, as her parents approached her apartment door. "Would you all quit worrying about me, please?"

"Honey, is everything okay?" Ann asked. "We heard you screaming. Why were you screaming so loud and for so long?"

"Mom, I just had a nightmare, that's all. I'll be fine. I just need for everyone to go back to bed." Sara looked down, trying to keep her hair in her face as much as possible so no one would see her cuts. She could feel the blood dripping from her hands, and she could swear she could hear it hitting the carpet in soft plunks.

She again assured everyone she was fine, closed the door, and headed directly for the bathroom. She stopped dead in her tracks just as she was about to open the door. What things were waiting for her behind the door, waiting to take her a little farther into a world of insanity that she was afraid she wouldn't be able to come back from? she thought.

She opened the door and found everything in its place. As she stood in front of the mirror, all Sara could think about was how she was going to explain this one. She could see several small cuts over her eyebrow and up her legs and arms. She would have to wear long sleeves and a turtleneck; she was thankful it was getting chilly outside, especially at night. She could make up something about the cuts on her face.

Sara took a blanket and laid on the couch. She left several lights on; she didn't feel safe anymore in the dark, and she never knew what or who was crawling out of or into things. She didn't have the energy to deal with it anymore.

The next day, Sara decided to work at home. With all the marks on her, and her mental state being so delicate, she thought it would be best; she didn't want to have to explain anything to anyone. Sara was getting dressed when someone knocked on her door.

"Just a minute," she yelled.

"Sara, it's only me. It's Mom."

"Hold on, Mom. I'll be right there," Sara yelled again. She quickly threw on jeans and a sweatshirt and headed for the front door. Her mom had a giant smile on her face when she entered the apartment, but as Sara turned to close the door and face her mom, Ann's face went as white as a ghost. Sara took her mom by the shoulders and asked her what was wrong, but Ann just stood there, expressionless, then bolted for the front door.

Sara followed her mom, not knowing what was going on, and watched helplessly as she tripped on the fourth step down and fell down the remaining stairs. Sara screamed as her father came out of the apartment, saw Ann on the ground, and knelt down to make sure his wife was okay.

"Honey, are you all right?" Bill asked gently. Ann looked up at Bill and said she was fine. Bill noticed her nose was bleeding. Sara quickly made it down the stairs and helped Bill get Ann off the floor. Ann looked at Sara and began to scream. It was a scream not even Bill had ever heard before.

"Mom, what's wrong?" Sara begged. "Tell me what's wrong!" Sara's mom was trying to run into her apartment and get away from Sara. Sara followed her parents into the apartment. Bill sat Ann on the couch and ran into the bathroom to get a cold rag. Sara sat beside her mom and told her to pinch her nose at the bridge and lean forward to stop the bleeding.

"Did you hurt anything else when you fell?" Sara asked.

"No, I'm fine. I just thought I saw something and must have lost my footing, that's all," she said, looking at Sara and Bill. "I'll be fine if you both would stop harping on me all the time.

"I'm sorry, Mom, but I want to take care of you, so you better get used to it," Sara said with a smile.

Sara then asked her mom what she saw, but Ann explained it away, saying all the excitement and the fatigue from the airplane ride must have gotten to her. Sara made her mom lie on the couch and went into the bedroom to get a blanket. Ann needed to get her rest.

Sara heard her phone ringing up in her apartment and headed for the door. "I need to get that. It could be my boss, and I'm working from home today. Will you and mom be okay?"

"Yes, we'll be fine. Go," Bill reassured his daughter, and she headed upstairs.

Ann looked at Bill and said, "Something is wrong here, seriously wrong. I'm scared to death."

"What do you mean, Ann? What's wrong?"

"I don't know yet, and I'm afraid to find out. I sense something is terribly wrong with our daughter. Sara seems distant and different to me somehow."

Bill assured his wife that Sara was fine, but Ann wasn't convinced. **Something was in the air, something in Sara's aura. She could feel it.**

Bill placed his arms around Ann and told her everything was going to be okay. Then he went to get some Motrin for Ann; he knew she was going to be very sore otherwise.

Ann and Bill heard a knock on their door. "Mom, Dad? Are you okay?" It was Sara.

"Come on in," Bill called. "We're fine."

"Mom, how are your nose and hip?"

"I'm going to be really sore tomorrow." Bill handed her the Motrin, and Sara walked into the kitchen and made an ice pack for her mom's nose.

"This will help," she said, handing the ice pack to Ann, "but you're going to have two black eyes tomorrow." Sara could already see the swelling getting worse and dark circles beginning to form around both of Ann's eyes. Sara had a slight grin on her face and noticed one beginning to form on Ann's face as well.

"Yeah, I'll be real pretty tomorrow," Ann said. "Everyone will think I was beat up or something."

"Mom, just tell them 'you should see the other guy.' " Sara put her arm around her mom's shoulder and gave her a kiss on cheek.

An hour later, after making sure her parents were okay, Sara went back to her apartment and decided to get some dinner for everyone. She called Tom and asked him if he wanted to take a walk with her to one of the many local restaurants, and he agreed. After picking up some Italian food, they sat down in her parents' apartment and ate a wonderful dinner of chicken Parmesan and pasta. Tom told Sara and Ann what a wonderful addition Bill would be with his knowledge of the construction business.

At 10 p.m., they decided to call it a night. They bid each other goodnight, and Tom and Sara went into their own apartments and prepared for sleep. Sara decided to take a hot bath. She put on water for tea, gathered her nightclothes, and lowered herself into the hot water. After a relaxing bath, she made herself a cup of tea and sat in front of her TV for a minute to catch the news. Then Sara went to bed and enjoyed an uneventful and uninterrupted sleep. When she woke up in the morning, she felt rested and wonderful. No matter what, she was going to have a good day.

THE MAN IN THE MIRROR

The next couple of days were so normal, Sara almost forgot about the weird things that had happened. Tom called one night to say hi and tell her he loved her; she returned the sentiment. He wanted to take her out to a movie when she got home, and she thought that was a wonderful idea. They had both been so busy lately, they had barely seen each other.

When Sara got home from work, she found Tom looking in the local paper to see what movie looked good. She stopped by her parents' apartment to say hello. Ann was in the kitchen fixing dinner, and Bill was in the bathroom getting ready to take a shower. Sara was talking with Ann when they heard a loud noise, like glass breaking on the bathroom floor. Ann and Sara ran to the bathroom and began to bang on the locked door, yelling for Bill to open it, but she got no answer.

Sara yelled to Ann, "Run next door and get Tom, quick!" She did as she was told, and Sara kept pushing on the door, hoping it would give way under her frame. After several attempts, it did, but the door wouldn't open all the way. Something was in the way on the floor. It was Bill, and he wasn't moving.

Sara looked up and saw a reflection in the mirror. A large man was standing behind the door with an axe in his hand. When Sara tried to reach in and touch the top of her dad's head, the door slammed shut. She pulled her arm out just in time and began to yell even louder. No response.

Sara managed to crack open the door again. The large man in the mirror was still there, looking at Sara. He was as white as a ghost, about six feet five inches tall, and of medium build. His clothing was old, dirty, and full of holes, and flesh hung off his hands. Maggots crawled all over him. He said in the creepiest voice Sara ever heard, "Don't get involved in things you know nothing about."

Sara just screamed, and when she turned around, Tom was there. Tom got in front of the door and pushed as hard as he could. He was able to move Bill and gain entrance. Tom yelled to Ann to call for an ambulance, and she ran for the phone. She dialed 911 but couldn't remember the address so she yelled for Sara. Sara took the phone from Ann and gave the 911 dispatcher the address. They were on the way, the dispatcher said.

Sara then rushed back to the bathroom. Bill was lying on the floor, naked and out cold. He had a gash in his head that was bleeding pretty badly. Glass covered the entire bathroom floor. Tom had covered him with a towel. Sara told Ann to go open the front door so the paramedics could get in. Just then, Bill became slightly more conscious and alert, and began to mutter a few words. The paramedics arrived moments later. Sara didn't say a word to anyone about what she saw, or rather what she *thought* she saw.

The paramedics loaded Bill onto the stretcher and told Sara what hospital they were taking him to. Tom pulled his car around and drove Sara and Ann to the hospital where Bill received 15 stitches in the back of his head and several in the palm of his right hand where he tried to break his fall. The doctor said he still needed to go for a scan of his head, but he thought he would be fine.

When Sara and Ann were allowed to see him, Bill was sitting up in the bed, and he swore someone had been in the bathroom with him. "That's why I fell," he said. "I was startled when a large man appeared through the glass shower door. He had an axe in his hand, and I was so scared, I tried to turn and get out, but I slipped on the soap and fell though the glass doors. I'll pay for the doors, Sara. I'm so sorry."

Sara just looked him and gave him a great big kiss on the cheek. "Don't be so silly, Dad," she replied. "I just care that you're okay." He assured her he was, except for a slight headache. Several hours and tests later, the hospital released Bill, and Tom drove everyone home. They had been up all night and were exhausted.

After Sara got her father settled on the couch, she went into the bathroom to clean up the glass. As she began to sweep, she saw something that confirmed what she had seen in the bathroom earlier. A maggot. The room also smelled like death that was recently present. Sara thought she was going to be sick, but she fought through it and finished cleaning up. She then went back into the living room to check on her dad. He was asleep and appeared comfortable.

Ann assured Sara and Tom that she would keep a close eye on Bill, but Sara didn't want to leave. She wanted to keep an eye on him herself; she had just gotten them back and didn't want to lose them. Sara kept thinking, Isn't this wonderful! My mom has two black eyes, and my dad has stitches. People are going to think I beat the two of them up.

Sara decided her parents would be okay, so she returned to her apartment and called her boss to tell him what had happened. When she told him she needed to work at home that day, her boss relayed his concern that all sorts of things seemed to be occurring to her lately. She assured him these were just fluke things and eventually everything would settle down. Things were getting back on track as far as she was concerned, and her work habits would get better.

After feeling scrutinized by her boss, Sara decided to go to bed. She didn't need any more of anybody's crap. Sara fell asleep almost instantly but was soon awakened by a nightmare. She dreamed she was lying on the ground with maggots crawling all over her. Every time she tried to scream, a few crawled into her mouth until it was full. She woke up screaming and covered in sweat. Sara got out of bed and walked into the kitchen, got a glass of water and some Tylenol, and took a deep breath, hoping she could sleep dream-free. Luckily, she did.

When she woke up, she called Tom. He had stayed home to keep an eye on Bill and do some paperwork to do. Tom had some workers coming over. Sara wanted to have the secret room remodeled and the metal staircase secured. Sara thought that it would be nice to have a different staircase put in and turn the secret room into a work spot for her dad. For Christmas she planned to get him a table saw and some tools to work with; Tom was going to help her find what she needed. The remodeling project would be expensive, but Sara felt it was going to be worth it. Tom's employees could get started right away, and he was going to supervise the work.

After getting dressed, Sara went downstairs to see how her dad was. He was sitting on the couch with a cup of coffee in one hand and the TV remote in the other. Sara walked over to him and gave him a kiss.

"Hey, Dad, how are you feeling?" she asked.

"Fine. I feel great. My headache is gone, and I'm not as sore as I was yesterday."

"That's wonderful! You had me worried."

"Sara, don't worry about me. That's what I have your mom for." Bill began to laugh, and Ann threw the dishtowel at him.

"Sounds like you two are more than okay," Sara said as she headed for the door. "I guess I don't need to babysit you. I think I'll run down to the office for a bit. When I get back we'll have dinner."

"Sara, you know you don't have to eat with us every night," her mom said.

"Are you telling me to stay home tonight?" she asked.

"Yes. Your dad and I want to spend some time together; you know we still do that every once in a while," Ann said with a smile and a wink.

"I got you," Sara said. "I'll spend some time tonight with Tom then. We really haven't spent much time together lately. Well, call me if you need anything. Oh, by the way, Tom's workers are going to be downstairs working on the staircase so it'll be noisy down there for a bit."

Sara picked up her briefcase and headed for her office, which was walking distance away. She loved being able to walk to work, especially on those really nice days. She did what she needed to do and headed home, stopping at the store and picking up groceries for a couple of days.

When she got home, she quickly changed into jeans and a T-shirt. She couldn't wait to see the progress the construction workers had made. Sara took her laundry and headed downstairs, figuring she might as well hit two birds with one stone. After getting her laundry started, she headed toward the secret room. All the books were in boxes over by the wall at the far end of the room. The large desk was sitting in the main basement. The metal staircase was gone and in its place was a frame where a normal staircase would take its place. The workers still had to add the actual steps, but most of the work was done. She was impressed at how quickly they were getting the job done. Sara was going to have a small enclosed doorway built so she could have easy access to the steps from the roof. She wanted to bring more furniture and maybe a small gas grill up there, so they could do some cooking out. She looked forward to having the doorway built as well.

THE TRAP DOOR

Sara bumped into the wooden stairframe and knocked a hammer to the ground. When the hammer hit the ground, it made a funny noise, as if it hit something hollow. Sara got on her hands and knees and started to clean away the dirt from the ground when her hand hit something hard. Sara decided to get a broom from the laundry area to sweep away all the loose dirt. She heard the upstairs door creak open, and a beam of light shone down the stairs.

Sara yelled, "Hello. Who's up there?"

"It's only me, Sara, Tom."

Sara breathed a sigh of relief. "Hey, I think I found something." Tom came down the stairs and greeted her with a long kiss.

"So what did you find now? You know, you're always finding things," he said with a loving smile.

"I think there's a trap door by the staircase. Want to help me uncover it?"

"Sure! I'm always up for an adventure," Tom said. Sara showed Tom how when she stomped on the ground, the sounds were different, and kept sweeping the dirt away. Soon she exposed a trap door with a flushed handle the dirt easily hid.

Tom said, "I bet you it's a canning cellar. They used to have these in just about every house."

Sara looked at Tom. "Boy, this house is just full of surprises, isn't it?"

Tom reached over and tried to pull open the trap door by its small handle, but had no luck. He told Sara he needed to get a crow bar or something to pry open the door with. Sara was starting to have second thoughts about the whole thing.

She was feeling very uneasy about that room. The little hairs on the back of her neck began to rise, and she could feel her hear begin to pound as fast as a hummingbird's. She felt dizzy and sweaty and immediately sat on the ground.

Tom returned with a crow bar and noticed Sara was as white as a sheet. "Sara, what's wrong?"

"I just didn't eat today and felt a little lightheaded, that's all." Tom put the crow bar down, picked Sara up, and carreried her to his apartment where he made her a sandwich and coffee. After 30 minutes, she told him she felt much better and wanted to go back down to the cellar. Since she looked better and he was curious himself, Tom agreed, and they headed back downstairs.

Tom took the crow bar and tried to use it as leverage to open the trap door, but he only managed to crack the wood. Tom walked over to the washer and retrieved the flashlight kept on a shelf above it, then got on his knees and ran the beam of light around the frame of the door.

Tom looked up at Sara and said, "I know why the door won't open."

"Why?" Sara replied.

"It's been nailed shut for some reason. Someone sure didn't want this door to ever be opened again."

Sara's uneasy feeling about the situation returned. "Tom, maybe we should just leave it. I mean, maybe something's down there. Somebody obviously didn't want this door to be found."

"Come on, Sara," Tom said, "don't tell me you're scared." Tom had a smile on his face, but Sara didn't.

"What the hell do you mean by that?" Sara said loudly, almost to the point of yelling.

"Nothing! I'm kidding with you is all," Tom replied. "If you don't want to see what's down there, we don't have to open it."

Sara looked at Tom apologetically. "I don't know why I'm so jumpy tonight. For some reason, I'm feeling very uneasy about this."

"Sara, with everything that's been going on here, it's natural that you're a little edgy, and spooked."

"I'm not spooked, okay?" Sara rebuked.

"Okay!" Tom replied. "You're not spooked. So, are we doing this or not?"

"Go ahead," Sara said. "Let's get this over with. I'm not going to sleep until I know what's down there, and I don't think you will either."

"You're right, I won't," replied Tom. "You know what happened to the cat, don't you?"

Sara kicked dirt in Tom's direction. "Very funny," she said.

"Speaking of which, how is old Ben these days?"

"He just lies around. Not much curiosity there. It's a dog's or cat's life, you know."

Tom chuckled, then took the rounded end of the crow bar and began removing one nail at a time. When Tom finished, he had removed 42 three-inch nails. He reached down and opened the trap door, setting off a cloud of dust and debris. When it settled, Tom and Sara saw a staircase that led down into just what Tom said, a canning cellar. Sara took her flashlight and headed cautiously down the stairs. On the second step from the bottom, she tripped and fell, landing on her back.

"Sara, Sara! Are you okay?" Tom yelled.

"Yeah, I'm okay. I just hurt my pride a little bit." Sara lay sprawled out as if she were ready to make dirt angels. The entire floor was covered with several inches of dirt, so Sara's fall wasn't as hard as it could have been.

Tom walked down the steps. "Sara, are you sure you're okay?"

"Yeah, I'm fine," Sara replied. "Ouch, I think I did some damage. Tom, I can't get up. What's wrong with me?"

"Sara, tell me where you're hurting," Tom said gently, kneeling down next to her.

"I have a big crack in my ass now." Sara began to laugh.

Tom stood up and, in a light yet sarcastic voice, said, "You're so funny, ha ha."

Sara pointed the beam of her flashlight directly under her chin and said, "Spooky, isn't it."

Tom extended his hand to help her up. Sara accepted it, and he pulled her up on her feet so fast and hard, she almost flew forwards.

"Tom, I forgot what a strong guy you are. You almost knocked me off my feet. Well, actually you did knock me off my feet, just not that way."

Tom aughed and said, "You should be a comedian. What kind of happy pill did you take, and why aren't you sharing?"

"I didn't take anything. I just think it's nice to laugh, you know?"

"It feels good," Tom agreed with a big chuckle.

Sara looked around and grew serious again. "What kind of house of horrors do you think we'll find down here?"

"It looks just like a simple canning cellar to me. What do you think?"

"No telling, with all the things that have been going on here. Nothing is simple."

Tom had a puzzled look on his face. "Sara, what are you talking about now?"

Sara turned around and looked directly at Tom. "What do you mean, what do I mean? I'm talking about all the crazy crap that's been going on in this house, between you and the cat, the funny smells, about the dreams I've been having."

"Okay, okay! I know what you're talking about. I was trying to make a joke. Calm down!"

Sara walked over to Tom and gave him a passionate kiss. "I'm sorry," she said. "I didn't know what you meant, or if you were insinuating that I'm crazy. If you said you absolutely didn't know what was going on here, I would have been sure I was going nuts."

"I know you're not crazy," Tom reassured her. "I haven't seen all the things you have, but something is definitely going on here. I know that.

"Well, as long as we understand each other," Sara said as she wrapped her arms around Tom's neck. He put his arms around her waist and they held onto each other.

As they stood there embracing, Sara saw something hanging in the corner of the cellar. She dropped her arms from around Tom's neck and walked toward what caught her eye. Tom followed. Sara began to stumble. Something very bumpy and loose was on the ground. Sara aimed the beam of light down and saw that she was walking on bones and skulls. Sara was so scared at this discovery that she lost her balance and fell, this time landing on her left wrist. The flashlight had fallen from her hand and landed five feet in front of her. In its beam, Sara saw she was face to face with some type of animal skull with hollowed eyes and long canines; it looked like the skull of a cat. Sara screamed and jumped to her feet; it was like looking at something from a horror movie, she thought.

In her fear and haste, she almost knocked Tom to the ground. She was screaming.

"Sara, calm down," Tom said, grabbing her by the shoulders. "Everything's going to be all right."

"Tom, what is this?" she asked.

"Stray animals must have gotten in here and were unable to get out," he explained.

Sara could smell the years of decaying carcasses. She hadn't noticed the smell when she first entered the room, but now it was very strong.

"Tom, do you smell that?" Sara asked him.

"It smells a little musky and damp, but that's about it. Why?" he asked.

"It smells horrible to me, and I didn't notice it before." Sara walked over and picked up the flashlight. "Tom, let's look for some kind of light switch. We need more light in here before something else happens."

Tom took the flashlight from Sara and aimed the beam of light at the ceiling, but he didn't see anything. The room, as far as he could tell, was small with all dirt floors. There were several rows of old wooden shelves along the windowless walls, and some had fallen over the years, probably under the weight of canned goods on them. Tom saw broken glass on the ground and figured the stray animals that had gotten into the room might have eaten the rotting vegetables just to survive, though most of them probably starved to death.

While Tom walked around, Sara stayed put. She really didn't want to know what else was in this room. All of a sudden, Tom hurried toward Sara, took her by the arm, and began guiding her up the narrow steps.

"Come on, Sara, we need to go, right now."

"Tom, what's wrong. What did you find? Tell me!" Sara cried as Tom began to push her up the narrow steps. Sara stopped and turned to look at Tom, stopping him in his tracks.

"Okay, Tom, that's enough. What's going on? What did you see?"

Tom didn't want to answer her. Sara took the flashlight from his hand and began to shine the beam of light over each wall. She stopped when she saw something light in color and slowly walked over to it. Sara clenched her hand to her mouth when she realized what it was: a skeleton hanging from a beam with a pile of clothes and an axe lying at its feet. As she circled the skeleton, Sara felt something hitting her left shoulder. When she spun around to see what it was, she got entangled in what appeared to be a second skeleton, only this one was much smaller, like that of a child, also with clothes at its feet. Both were hanging by a four-inch thick rope around their necks. Sara became paralyzed, unable to move; she couldn't even scream. She just looked at Tom, not knowing what to do next.

"Come on, we need to call the police," Tom said. They headed to Tom's apartment and made the call. Within fifteen minutes, the police had cordoned off the area with the familiar yellow tape, and nobody was allowed downstairs. A Sergeant Allen came up to talk to Sara.

"Well, these two have been dead for a long time," he said. "The crime scene investigators are estimating the style of clothing to be somewhere in the 1920s. It's amazing nobody found them before this."

Sara told the sergeant she had recently bought the apartment building and found several rooms that hadn't been used for a long time. She didn't even know this one existed until just a little while ago. She explained how she dropped the hammer and it made a different type of noise; that's how she found the room. Sgt. Allen also told her about the things they found in some of the jars that were on the shelves, and that the remains on the floor were canine and feline in nature.

When Sara pressed him for details, Sgt. Allen said, "We can't disclose that at this time."

"I really need to know now!" Sara insisted. "This is my building, and if anything else bad was found, you need to tell me!" Sara's voice had risen to a low yell, and Sgt Allen told her to calm down. There was so much activity in the apartment building, Sara felt confused about everything. She needed answers.

Sgt Allen told her they found what appeared to be fetuses in large canning jars behind some canned fruit. He wasn't sure what they were preserved in, but they had been there a long time. The next few days would tell them a lot after they ran their tests. Sara couldn't believe what she was hearing. There were dead babies in her house.

"Sergeant, do you know what they died from?"

"No, we won't know that until the coroner does autopsies."

After several hours, the police had found ten fetuses in jars, two skeletal remains, and many unidentified bones. Reporters were everywhere asking questions. Sara gave them a very brief statement, telling them she had lived there for a very short period of time and the remains were found purely by accident. She knew nothing about them until she and her tenant found a secret room after having some construction done.

During the next several days, Sgt. Allen made several visits to Sara's apartment. He told her the medical examiner stated the larger skeleton was male, approximately mid-thirties to mid-forties, and the other was that of a young woman, possibly twelve to twenty.

"Sara, they did have one thing in common," he said. "They both had the same DNA makeup, so they were related. I don't even know how to go about trying to solve this case. It could have been a murder/suicide type of incident, but we'll never know. They died 80-plus years ago. One thing bothers me, though. Some of those babies in the jars, well, some of them were fresh."

"What do you mean fresh?" Sara asked in alarm.

"As in less than 40 years old."

Sara didn't know what to say. Her eyes got big and filled with. How could someone do something so terrible to little babies?

"The medical examiner is still running tests, trying to see if any of them died of natural causes or if they were put in those jars still alive," the sergeant said.

"I can't believe someone could do something like that."

"Sara," Sgt. Allen said, "how long have you lived here?"

"Several months now. Why?"

"No reason. Just wondering, that's all."

"What about the previous owners?"

"No, I already looked into that. The last owner was an old lady who passed away in her sleep, and the person you bought the house from was a stepdaughter who was named executor of her estate. Everything that was sold was in her sister's name. I guess she and her sister also bought the house just down the street, but it's really run down now, and it definitely needs a new paint job. I'm sure you've walked passed it; it's a big pink house. You can't miss it."

Sara just about dropped her cup of coffee on the ground. She certainly knew that house, but she didn't dare say anything. The police officer noticed her hands were shaking.

"Sara, what's wrong?" he asked her.

"The whole idea that someone was killing babies and storing them in my apartment house just makes me a little nervous and uneasy. How would you feel?"

"I'm sorry if I offended you. I didn't mean to."

Sara was now feeling very depressed and confused. She didn't know what to think or what she would find out next. It seemed everything was circling back to Polly whose diary she found in the secret room. She thought she had seen Polly with a woman in the first secret room. This woman was lying on the desk with her legs raised as if she were having a gynecological exam except Polly was performing some kind of procedure on her. Sara knew what it was: an illegal abortion. Sara had read about the age of women suffrage when they fought for women's rights to birth control. Sara remembered reading how using contraception was illegal back in those days, and women did whatever it took to keep from having children they couldn't afford. They went through these procedures without the use of any antiseptic or anesthesia, and many died of infection or blood loss. Sara thought Polly must have tried to help some of these women, but she also wondered how many women Polly may have killed. In that secret room, did Polly feel the need to keep all the aborted babies in jars or just those that had some kind of significance? Sara didn't care what the reason was, it was sick in her eyes, and she felt a little spooked that it happened in her house.

When the medical examiner's report came back, it showed several of the jarred fetuses died of traumatic removal. "That means they were forcibly removed from their mothers' wombs and deliberately placed in jars," explained Sgt. Allen.

Sara felt more disturbed than ever and wasn't sure she even wanted to live in her dream house that now was her nightmare. Sara loved her new home and really didn't want to move, but she didn't want to stay at the expense of her sanity; that meant more to her than any home. She had living proof of that in her mom. Sara remembered coming home from school and finding her mom hiding in a closet or under the bed, telling her people were out to get her. Sometimes she had a knife next to her. That's when Sara knew her mom was getting ready to go back into the hospital. Things got really bizarre, and her mom started talking a mile a minute and not making any sense. She would also cock her head to try and hear the voices she swore she was hearing.

As Sara got older, her mom was getting sicker, and her hospital stays were longer. Sara remembered the last time she saw her mom before she left for college. Ann became enraged at one of the neighbors and attacked her with a knife. Sara didn't remember what the fight was about, but she sure remembered the fight Ann put up when the cops and ambulance people came. Her mom screamed at the top of her lungs about making sure a cat didn't follow her, because it was trying to kill her. She tried to kill the neighbor's cat with the knife, but it managed to escape.

The cat looked like Ben. It was a large white alley cat named Stinker that belonged to her friend Heather. She and Sara would play dress-up with the cat who was always so cooperative and friendly. Sara and Heather would dress the cat in bonnets and baby sweaters, and it always looked so pretty even though it was a male.

When her mom was at her worst, she didn't even recognize her daughter, and that's what scared Sara the most. She remembered her mom's eyes when she became enraged and the one vein on her forehead that seemed to grow as her anger grew. Sara never knew what her mom would do, and she didn't want to get killed by her own mother. Sara understood her mom had an illness, but her dad seemed to ignore it sometimes. Sara knew when her mom was ready for a hospital stay, but her dad seemed to wait until she attacked someone and then he got scared. Things got worse when Sara left for college.

Bill finally put Ann back into the hospital, and they started her on new medication. It worked like a charm to manage her anger along with her hallucinations and trips to the hospital. Ann became more productive and could finally keep a job without getting fired. She was able to take care of herself much better, and her violence was almost nonexistent. That's when Sara asked her parents to come and live with her. Ann's doctor gave her a good referral for a psychiatrist in California.

Now they were settling in, but what were they settling into? Sara was experiencing all these crazy things, and she wondered if her mom had felt the same way. Was it like this when her mom had seen and heard things? Did things feel as real to her mom as they did to her? If her mom felt this scared, how did she have the courage to come back every time and try again?

Sara wondered if she needed to be on medication, just like her mom. A simple anti-anxiety medication might do nicely. Maybe a cocktail of antidepressants and antipsychotics was her ticket to sanity. Sara needed an emotional vacation. She quickly dismissed this line of thought and decided to be strong; she needed to deal with everything that was going on and get on with her life.

Sgt. Allen had let her know the case was closed. The medical examiner and police determined the two skeletons found in her basement weren't worth investigating; no one knew what happened, and they would never know. The ME also determined the fetuses were dead before they were placed in the jars more than eighty years ago, and they all were under 18 weeks of gestation, so they appeared to be aborted fetuses.

Even though the case was closed, Sara felt uneasy about the house now. Just knowing that people were killed and hung in that hidden room gave her the creeps. She wanted to forget the whole thing, so when Tom came over that nighjt after work, she flew into his arms, giving him a big kiss and hug.

"Let's go out for dinner tonight, just you and me," Tom suggested after kissing her again.

"That sounds wonderful," Sara responded.

"Give me an hour or so to get a shower and shave and then we'll go."

"Okay, perfect. I need to do the same."

Sara headed for her bedroom, picked out some clothing, and hopped in the shower. The phone rang, but Sara decided to let the answering machine pick it up. After she got dressed, she headed to the phone to see who called. The female caller said, "Hi, Sara. I asked you very nicely to stop meddling, but you refused to listen. Now you're going to pay dearly, and so will your family. I know what your mom's problems are; I will make sure your mom has more problems than she ever had.

She's going to pay for your mistakes, and so will your boyfriend."

Sara placed the receiver back onto the cradle and just stood there, tears rolling down her face. Who was trying to torture her so much, and why? What did she do to deserve this in her life? Sara hit the save button. She wanted Tom to hear the message and then the police. Someone was out to get her and her family, and it wasn't just happening in her imagination.

When Tom came to the door, Sara led him over to the answering machine. "I want you to hear something," she said. "A woman just called me and left me this message. Someone is out to get me and my family, and you, too." Sara hit the play button, but the only message was from a long distance carrier asking her if she was happy with her phone service. Sara just looked at Tom, not knowing what to say.

"What happened to the message?" he asked.

"I don't know. Maybe it was nothing," she replied, sounding defeated and feeling crazy all over again. Tom knew something wasn't right and wanted to get her away from it all for a while.

"Let's go get that dinner," he said gently.

"Yeah, just a minute. Let me get my purse," she replied in a low, unsure tone.

SARA'S BOSS

After the last several months and everything that had happened, Sara was having some problems at work. One morning her boss pulled her into his office and asked her what was going on. Sara assured him she was fine and her work would improve now that her parents were settling in. But her boss wasn't convinced. He asked her about the scratches and other injuries he had noticed on her several months ago. She assured him again they were all just accidents, but she got the distinct impression that he was insinuating that maybe her new boyfriend was getting rough with her.

Sara felt embarrassed about the whole situation and tried to make light of it. "Just all unfortunate accidents," she said again. "My mom and dad have had a few accidents themselves, and Tom had nothing to do with any of those either."

"Sara, what's really going on with you? You're usually so attentive about your briefs and lately, they have been incomplete and frankly incoherent at times. Are you sure you're feeling okay?" he asked.

Sara started to feel angry about what he was implying. Did he think she was crazy? If he really knew what was going on in her life, he would understand and possibly wonder why she hadn't gone crazy earlier. Sara knew her work was slipping. She just didn't realize how much until her boss pointed it out. For the next couple weeks, Sara buckled down and concentrated mainly on her work. Tom called her several times to take her out, but she declined. One night Tom stopped by with take-out and forced her to take a break. As they sat at the kitchen table eating Chinese food and sipping on red wine, Tom couldn't help but feel worried. Sara looked frail and thin.

"Are you eating and sleeping enough?" he asked.

"Yes, it's just that I have so much work to do, I just can't stop."

"You need to take care of yourself, Sara, or you won't be any good to yourself or your parents, and might even lose your job. Besides, I miss you."

Sara gave him a hug and asked, "Why are you so good to me? Why do you love me?"

Tom replied with a gentle kiss on the forehead. "I love you because you're the most special woman I've ever known. You're sweet and loving and you're who you are. How's that for an answer?"

Sara replied, "I love it, and I love you, Tom, so much." The exchanged passionate kisses and Tom headed home, reassured that Sara was okay. He knew she had a lot of work to do, and he didn't want her to get fired. Jobs like hers didn't come around that often, and he knew how much she liked what she did.

Sara knew she lucked out when she got the job, which is why she needed to prove herself to her boss. After a couple weeks of keeping her nose to the grindstone, her boss said, "Sara, I'm glad to see you back; you seem to be your old self once more."

"Thank you," Sara said. "I'm sorry I fell behind and don't plan on it happening again."

"How are your parents adjusting to this new town?"

"They are doing well after that whole hospital thing with my dad; they're both being more careful and my dad's working a lot with Tom. I still worry about my mom being alone, but she seems okay. Thanks for asking."

"Well, I want to make sure my number one lawyer is happy," her boss said with a smile.

"Thank you, Mr. Hall, for being so understanding, and I promise I won't let you down." Sara went back to her office and sat down at her desk for a moment; trying to get herself back on track. Sara stared at the computer screen. Blank, just a blue screen. She opened her top drawer to retrieve some papers and found something strange. A yellow legal pad with words written all over the paper, up, down, and sideways, all in her handwriting: KILL THEM ALL, FIRST YOUR MOM AND DAD, THEN TOM, THEN YOUR PUSHY, ASSHOLE BOSS AND ANYONE ELSE WHO GETS IN YOUR WAY. It also said "AND THAT STINKING CAT" in larger, bolder print than the other words, as if to stand out.

Sara just sat there, stunned. She didn't remember writing anything like that. No, she *wouldn't* write anything like that, but it was in her handwriting. Was someone trying to play a cruel joke on her? Were her parents' and Tom's lives in danger?

She noticed the second page had drawings on it. Drawings of people handing by the neck from, expressions of horror on their faces; knives dripping with blood; dismembered body parts. Sara was horrified. Was someone in her office when she was out? Did someone want her to go crazy? Her co-workers didn't know what was really going on in her apartment building. Whoever did this would pay, and pay dearly; she would make sure of that. Sara walked over to her boss's office and knocked on the door.

"Come on in," he called.

"Has anyone used my office while I've been away?" Sara asked.

"Not that I know of," Mr. Hall answered. "Is anything wrong? Is anything missing?"

"Oh, no. Things just look and feel different, probably because I haven't been here. Thanks." Sara went back to her office, not sure what to do next. She opened her last drawer and gasped at what she found. A doll that looked very old, covered in what appeared to be red paint. It had a note attached around its neck that said "BABY KILLER," and there was a small letter opener stuck into its vaginal area.

Sara grabbed the doll and threw it in the trash. Afraid someone might see it if she left it there, she then wrapped the doll in the white plastic trash bag and laid it in her briefcase. She would take it home and get rid of it there where she wouldn't have to explain anything to anyone. Things had been so quiet and now this.

On her walk home from work, Sara decided to stop at the store and pick up some needed groceries. She had to walk past the pink house, which looked even more run down and creepy than the last time she was there. Sara was walking slow, looking up at the house, and almost fell on a crack in the sidewalk. The house was talking to her again, trying to draw her in, only this time she wouldn't let it happen. She just ignored humming noise she heard in her head and continued to walk. Then she got a sudden and excruciating pain in her head, as if the house was yelling at her for walking past.

Sara began to walk as fast as she could, holding on to her head. By the time she got home, she felt better. She went around the back and put the white trash bag into the garbage, glad to get rid of it. When she got upstairs, she called Tom and invited him to dinner . He accepted. Then she walked downstairs and knocked on her parents' door..

"Hey, Mom." Sara gave Ann a kiss on the check when she answered the door. "How's everything going?"

"Wonderful," she answered. "How was your day?"

"Good. I'm getting caught up with everything, and it's going well. Listen, I'm having Tom over for dinner. Do you and Dad want to join us?

"No, thanks, sweetheart. I've got dinner made already, and your dad's in the shower, I think he's just going to want to relax tonight. I appreciate you asking. You and Tom should enjoy the evening alone."

"I love you, Mom. Say hi to Dad for me. I'll see you later, okay?" Sara said, giving her mom a hug. As she headed up the stairs toward her apartment, Amber was coming down the stairs.

"Hey, you. When did you get back?"

"Just yesterday," Amber answered.

"How did your shoot go?"

"Wonderful. We're on a break for a rewrite."

"Well, it seems like everyone could use a break lately."

"Hey, I saw what you did down in the basement. It looks wonderful. I also heard what they found. That's kind of creepy."

"Yeah, it was, but things seem to be settling down a little bit. How long are you home for?"

"I'm not sure," Amber answered. "Sometimes these things can take a few weeks or maybe a couple of months. Anyway, I'll see you later; I'm late for a date tonight."

"Okay. Do you want to get together tomorrow for drinks, maybe dinner?" Sara asked. Amber was a little reluctant after what happened the last time she and Sara had dinner, but she agreed anyway and told her she would see her tomorrow.

"Oh, by the way, did those clothes I gave your mom fit her?" Amber asked as she headed out the door.

"Perfectly," Sara said with a grin that made Amber feel uncomfortable. Sara seemed different, not as friendly as she used to be. Something was going on, and Amber wasn't sure she wanted to know what it was.

When Sara entered her apartment, Ben was standing on top of her counter, meowing and wanting his dinner. Sara opened a can of tuna, and Ben devoured it as if he hadn't eaten in a week. Sara went to the bathroom and hopped in the shower.

Things seemed to be tense with everyone in the building—her parents, Tom, Amber. When Sara came back with Tom from the traumatic trip to the inn, Amber had locked Ben in the basement with his food and litter box. Amber had no explanation other than she felt like she was having an allergic reaction to him so she put him where Sara was going to leave him originally. She didn't think Sara would mind, and she didn't. What upset Sara was the way Amber told her, as if she cared less about Sara's reaction.

Sara's parents were also acting strangely toward her. Sara felt they were trying to avoid her. A few times when Sara walked down the steps to go visit, she heard movement in the apartment. But when she knocked, no one would answer the door. When she asked her parents if they wanted to go to dinner or something, they always seemed to have something else to do. Sara felt like she was being brushed aside and ignored for some reason, and she wasn't sure what to do about it.

Even Tom was acting strangely toward her. She would call his cell phone and get only his voice mail. He never seemed to be home anymore, and when he was, he always had paperwork to do. She was glad he was coming over tonight so she could talk to him about it.

Sara felt things were really settling down since the removal of all those jars with the babies in them and the skeletons. She hadn't had any more nightmares or smelled any offensive odors. She was gaining psychological strength and wanted to enjoy life with Tom and her parents. Sara felt better and stronger than ever. Things also started getting back on track with everyone in the apartment building. Tom began to answer his cell phone again, and she saw her parents more often. Amber seemed to lighten up as well. Sara felt like everything was going to be all right.

One Sunday morning, she thought it would be fun for everyone to go out for breakfast together. There was a nice family restaurant several blocks away, it was a bright, sunny morning, and they could walk. Everyone agreed, and they had a wonderful breakfast and enjoyed each other's company.

On the way home, they got to the corner of her block and proceeded to walk across the street when a speeding car came out of nowhere and knocked Ann to the ground. The mirror on the vehicle caught her in the left hip, and Ann went down, screaming in agony. The driver didn't stop, but Sara was able to get a partial plate number. At the hospital, it was determined Ann had a broken hip and would require surgery to repair it. The surgery was scheduled for the next morning, and Sara was going to make sure she was there.

"Come on, Sara, I'll take you home." Tom said. "Bill's going to stay with your mom tonight, and I'll drive you here in the morning."

"I really don't want to leave," said Sara, trying not to lose it.

"Listen, you can't do anything right now," Tom said gently. "Your mom needs her rest, and your dad's here. If anything happens, your dad will call you."

"Tom," said Sara, tears running down her cheeks, "I love my mom so much, and I don't want anything to happen to her."

"Sara, your mom's in good hands. She's got excellent nursing care, and the doctors here are the best. Everything is going to be okay. I promise."

Tom kissed her gently on the forehead. "Come on, you're exhausted."

Sara looked down at her watch. It was midnight, and they had been at the hospital for over 15 hours. Sara said goodbye to her mom, who assured her she would be walking again before she knew it. Sara gave her dad a kiss and told them both she would be back in the morning. She walked out of her mom's hospital room only to walk into a cop.

"Hi," he said. "I just wanted you to know we found the person responsible for hitting your mom today. His name is David Ads, and he's 21. Apparently he had been out all night clubbing and was completely wasted on alcohol and cocaine. We found him sitting in his car with the engine still running. We could see where he hit your mom by the mirror damage. We arrested him; his alcohol level was five times the legal limit. He couldn't even get out of his car without falling over. We don't even know how he drove without killing someone."

Sara looked at the cop and said angrily, "He almost killed my mom. That's close enough. I hope he goes to jail for a very long time!"

"Well, apparently he has two other drinking and driving convictions on his record, which guarantees a substantial amount of jail time."

"Which is no less than he deserves," Sara said. "Thanks for coming to let us know, Officer."

The officer left, and Tom took Sara home to his apartment. He poured them each a glass of wine and sat on the couch. Within a half-hour, they were both asleep, exhausted from the day's events.

At some point, Tom's phone began to ring. He opened his eyes to find a dimly lit apartment and Sara asleep on his arm. The caller was Bill saying Ann had taken a turn for the worse, and he and Sara needed to get her as soon as possible. Apparently Ann threw a blood clot that went into her lung. The doctors said that sometimes happens when someone has a traumatic bone break.

Tom woke Sara, told her briefly what was going on, and they rushed back to the hospital. Sara started to cry uncontrollably the minute she walked into the intensive care unit and saw her mom. Ann was as pale as a ghost. She had a tube down her throat to help her breathe, and she was on some medications to help keep her blood pressure down. The nurses said they thought she would eventually be fine, with time and faith. Hopefully God will give her more time, Sara thought. She wasn't ready to lose her mom yet.

Sara stayed by her mom's bedside and urged her dad to go home, change his clothes, take a shower, and get some sleep so he didn't get sick himself. Tom drove Bill home where they both followed Sara's orders and were back at the hospital.

Tom drove Sara home so she could do the same. He laid on Sara's couch to take a nap while Sara showered and changed. She was putting on a kettle of water for tea when the phone rang. It was Bill with good news.

"Your mom is breathing on her own, and she is going to be fine," Bill exclaimed. "They're going to do her hip surgery now, before they take out the breathing tube, so stay home, get some rest, and come back in the morning, okay? I'll call you when she's out of surgery."

"If anything happens, will you call me right away? I'll be right here," Sara said, not at all sure whether she should stay home or return to the hospital.

"I will absolutely call you if anything changes. I promise, honey."

Sara replied. "Dad, I love you. Give Mom a kiss for me, and tell her I love her, too, okay?"

"I sure will. Now, get some rest."

Sara hung up the phone and made her tea. She walked over to the couch where Tom was snoring loudly. Sara gently shook him, and he awoke with a start.

"What's wrong?" he said as he jumped up.

"Everything's fine. Relax." Sara told Tom everything, and he gave her a big hug. As he held her and reassured her everything would be okay, Sara told him to go to his apartment.

"Sara, don't you want me here with you?"

"I love you, Tom, but I really just need to go to bed and sleep. I'm sorry, honey."

"I understand," Tom said, and kissed Sara on the tip of her nose. "What time do you want to be at the hospital tomorrow?"

"Early in the morning. How about eight?"

"You got it. See you in the morning," Tom said.

Sara shut and locked the door behind Tom, finished her tea, and went straight to bed. For the first time in months, she had a nightmare. She dreamed she walked into her mom's hospital room and found Ben sitting on Ann's chest with something in his mouth. He dropped his prize and began to swat at it as if it were a toy. Then the cat turned to Ann and, with both claws, reached and pulled the breathing tube out of her mouth. Ann sat straight up and, with one last gasp, fell back into the bed dead. Nurses and doctors came running in and tried to save her mom but to no avail. Then they turned on Sara, asking her how the tube came out. Sara told them about Ben, but they didn't believe her, and she was arrested for the murder of her mom.

Sara bolted out of bed, knocking herself out of her nightmare. She looked around, almost forgetting she was in her own apartment and in her own bed. She went into the kitchen and got a drink of water. As she was drinking it, she noticed Ben playing with something on the floor. When she reached down to pick it up, Ben swatted her hand away as if he didn't want her to see it. She managed to get it away from him anyway. It was a plastic identification bracelet, the kind they give you in the hospital. It had her mom's name on it, along with drops of dried blood.

Sara panicked and called the hospital. The nurse said her mom was fine and that she actually had improved in the last couple of hours. But Sara wouldn't rest easy until she saw her mom for herself, so she got dressed and hopped into a cab.

When she got to the hospital, she found her dad asleep in the family waiting room. Her mom still had the tube in her throat, but she was awake.

Sara reached down to kiss Ann on the cheek and noticed a small clump of white hair on the bed. It looked like Ben's hair. She took Ann by the left wrist. No ID band. She walked over to the other side of her bed and looked at her right wrist. No band there either. She knew her mom had had a band—she saw the nurse put it on. And it was on her left wrist, Sara remembered. Sara looked at her mom's left wrist again, and saw a large scratch with dried blood.

While Sara was standing there, trying to figure out how and why Ben got into her mom's hospital room, the nurse came in and gave Sara an update. She said her mom did well with the surgery. The doctors fixed the break without any complications, and they should be able to take the tube out in a couple of hours. Sara was relieved, yet at the same time, she now feared for her mom's health and well-being. She figured this was just another dream. She must have taken the ID bracelet home by accident where Ben got hold of it. Maybe she got Ben's hair on her from Sara's clothes. That had to be what happened.

Just then, the nurse reentered the room and placed a new bracelet on Ann's left wrist. "Somehow her last one got lost so I'm just replacing it," the nurse explained.

"Thanks," Sara said to her as she held her mother's hand. A moment later, Bill entered the room. He had awoken from his nap and come to check on Ann, who was trying to talk with the tube still in place. The ventilator started making an awful noise, and the nurse returned. She pressed some buttons and silenced the machine for only seconds before it went off again.

"Is there a problem?" Sara asked the nurse, concerned for her mom.

"No," the nurse reassured her. "Your mom is just waking up and that's what happens; they start fighting the ventilator. It's nothing to be concerned about."

The nurse leaned over and told Ann to try to calm down. "She probably feels like she can't breathe, but it's just the tube, and it will hopefully come out soon, but she needs to calm down first."

Several hours later the doctor came in and removed the tube. Ann was still weak and unable to speak; her throat was very sore, and she needed some time to adjust. When she could talk, Ann told Sara about this horrible dream she'd had. She dreamed Ben was in the room and, for some reason, he was scratching at her left wrist. She didn't know why, and she couldn't see what was going on; her hands were tied down. She said she dreamed Ben was chewing on her tube, trying to dislodge it with his paws. She also dreamed that he managed to get the tube out, and she could feel herself drifting off to somewhere. She didn't know where, but she knew she wasn't coming back. She tried to scream, but nothing came out.

At this point Ann had tears in her eyes. "Sara, I didn't want to leave you or Dad."

"Mom, it was just a dream. Dad and I wouldn't let anything happen to you, not like that. I promise."

Ann just looked at Sara and said, wide-eyed with fear, "It was the most realistic dream I've ever had. I've never dreamed like that before in my life."

"Maybe it was all the medication you were given. They say you have some crazy dreams when you're under the knife."

The nurse brought in some juice and Jell-O for Ann, which made her feel much better, though she just wanted to sleep and wanted everyone to go home and do the same.

They all kissed her goodbye, and Tom drove them all back to the apartment building. Bill said goodnight to Sara, as did Tom. He needed to take a shower and get some sleep because he had a big client coming over to one of his new job sites and needed to be as rested at possible.

Sara wished him luck and said she would speak with him soon. She had some of her own work to do as well, like pay some bills and finish some paperwork for her boss. She didn't need to lose her job on top of everything else that was happening. This was a once-in-a-lifetime chance, and she was already walking on a tight rope with her boss.

The next morning, Sara decided to go to the library to see if she could find out any information on that pink house. When she got there, a woman with blonde hair and very striking green eyes asked her if there was something she could help her with. Sara asked her where she could find old newspaper clipping from the turn of the century. The lady immediately directed her toward a room on the third floor where they kept all of the old clipping on microfilm.

Sara headed upstairs to the microfilm room and sat down at one of the machines. She started her search by dates and came up with too many articles to go through, so she narrowed her search to articles that involved crime and women. Bingo, she found what she was looking for. There was an article about Polly being caught by her husband with her daughter in a house that was known to be performing illegal abortions. Apparently, her husband Henry attacked her, and she fought back, causing some serious injuries to Henry and landing herself in jail for six months. Sara knew from her sightings that Henry had been abusing her for a long time. Henry was a big guy, Polly was a small woman, and she must have been at her limit if she hurt him enough to land herself in jail. It must have taken everything she had.

The article read: 'Polly Mills, a 38-year-old female was arrested on Friday, March 3, after she attacked her husband Henry and almost killed him with an axe. Henry apparently heard rumors from neighbors that his wife was involved in some illegal activities. He followed her to a friend's house, and found her and their daughter Samantha, 16, in the basement assisting in an illegal abortion, two blocks away from their residence. After Henry became outraged and tried to get both back to his residence, a fight ensued, and both women began beating Henry. Polly took an axe and attacked her husband with it. Henry agreed to drop the charges after six months, and Polly was set free promising to be less insubordinate and more obedient toward her spouse.'

The article said Henry had Samantha by the hair, and Polly struck him in the back of the head with the axe; he never saw it coming. He was laid up for six weeks with a head wound, and Polly was compared to Lizzie Borden. Samantha was not charged with any crime—she was only an innocent bystander. But she did get a stern talking-to by the judge for being where she was. The judge blamed Polly and awarded full custody to Henry after he filed for divorce.

Sara flipped through dozens of articles before she came across an article stating that Henry stopped the divorce proceeding. Hundreds of people wrote him letters in protest because of the activity Polly was involved in, but he didn't have the heart to continue; he still loved Polly very much. Another article said that after Polly was released, she disappeared, never to be seen again. When the neighbors were questioned on whether or not she was ever seen in the neighborhood, they said no. The police searched Henry's house several times because if he claimed to love her so much, he would most certainly hide her from the police, who wanted to keep an eye on the potentially dangerous woman. The neighbors did tell the reporters Henry and his daughter moved away right after Polly was put in jail to avoid embarrassment. Apparently Henry was losing a lot of business because of her. No one wanted to do business with a man whose wife was in jail and then escaped, for fear she was out for revenge.

After another twenty minutes of flipping through the microfilm, Sara came across an article asking for any information regarding Henry and Samantha. Apparently both had disappeared as well and were never heard of again. The papers speculated that maybe Polly had indeed gotten her revenge.

As Sara sat there wondering what had happened to them, she flipped through more microfilm and found what she was looking for. Samantha reappeared at the age of 18 and got the entire estate estimated at about a million dollars. She apparently moved back into the old house along with her aunt and a cousin, who she had been living with since Henry went abroad. The aunt's name was Helen. She was much heavier than Polly and had a head full of graying hair. Everyone accepted her for who she said she was and never asked questions.

They lived in that house for another year and then Samantha moved away, presumably to live with her father. Helen stayed in the house. Samantha handed everything over to her for some unknown reason before she left. Helen transferred all the money into her own accounts. She didn't want to have to answer to anyone, said the article

As for Samantha, nobody really knew what happened to her. But Sara did. The evidence was apparent when she found them both hanging in her canning cellar. Sara believed Helen or Polly or both killed them to keep them quiet and steal the money, continue doing the illegal abortions, and live responsibility free.

Sara got home and decided to finish up the work she had to do for her boss. Several hours later she faxed everything over and decided to take a nap before dinner. She walked into the bathroom and noticed something gray, red, and disgusting on her bathroom rug. Sara bent down to take a closer look; it looked like hair, bone, and blood. It was a partially regurgitated rodent, on her forty-dollar rug, courtesy of Ben. She rolled up the rug and headed outside with it, dumping its contents a trash can. Then she headed for the laundry room. Sara's dad had clothes in the washer that were done; he was just waiting for the dryer to complete its cycle. Sara decided to go back upstairs and get a book to read; she would wait until her dad's things were done drying and throw the other stuff in for him.

Sara headed back downstairs after she retrieved her book, sat on the couch, and began to read. She dozed off and was awakened 30 minutes later by screams. Sara jumped up and began looking around, trying to find where the screams were coming from. They were coming from the canning cellar. Sara took the flashlight she kept on the ledge at the top of the basement stairs and headed for that room. With her heart in her throat from fear, she cautiously opened the hatch that led to the cellar and began descending the stairs. Instead of the screams, she heard a woman softly sobbing, which eased her fears a bit. She had the flashlight in her hand and was moving it back and forth motion to see if she could see anything. In the corner stood Polly. Next to her was Henry, hanging from the beams by his neck. His face was blue and black and very bloated; his skin was splitting, and black ooze began spilling out. Samantha was kneeling next to him with her hands tied behind her and her mouth covered with a single strip of white cloth. She was crying, and the gag had muffled her screams.

Polly stood over her with a large rope in one hand and an axe in the other. She placed the rope around Samantha's neck and, in one swoop, pulled on the rope and Samantha went airborne, kicking and trying to scream. Sara could see she was fighting for every last breath. Polly then proceeded to tie the rope around Henry's body. She then picked up the axe and struck Samantha in the back of the head. Samantha stopped moving; she was dead.

Sara couldn't take any more. She ran over to Samantha and tried to lift her body, but instead just got nothing but air. She kept trying, but nothing. Was this just a bad nightmare? No, it had seemed so real. Why would her own mother kill her? Samantha couldn't have done anything to deserve to be killed. How could Polly be so evil? Then Sara remembered the articles she read and all the money Henry left Samantha. Polly killed her husband and child over money.

All at once, Sara saw the diary she looked for and couldn't find. It just appeared on the ground in front of her. She went over and picked it up. When she turned around, everything was gone. Sara felt that Polly was trying to tell her what happened and why she did what she did. Sara didn't care why. She just couldn't believe a mother could kill her own child. She had to have been mentally ill. Sara remembered a few times when her own mother had psychotic episodes, how nutty she got, and how scared Sara sometimes was for her own safety.

Sara went back to her apartment and sat down on the couch, diary in hand. She wanted to read it, but she was most certainly afraid of what she was going to find out. She knew she was not dreaming, and that she'd had enough of Polly and her damn games. She went into the kitchen, put on a pot of coffee, and fed the cat. She didn't want any distractions when she read the diary.

Annette Johnson

When she saw the first page, she remembered seeing its contents before; it was a list of gifts from Polly and Henry's wedding day and who she received them from. Nothing too exciting, she thought, as she skimmed through other pages. Just everyday happenings, appointments, and a list of people or visitors that came.

There was an entry on March 10, 1915, that caught Sara's eye. The entry was very hard to make out; the ink appeared to be fading. The entry seemed to say something about Henry not wanting to perform his husbandly duties. He most likely had a girlfriend or mistress like most men did back in those days.

Polly also wrote that Samantha was sick a lot and that she had the doctor visit on more than one occasion. Sara wondered what was wrong with Samantha. Back then so many things could kill you, not like today where there were cures for so many of these illnesses.

Sara then found an entry made six months before Polly went to prison. She wrote that she began to help a neighbor who did things to help mostly poor women but some with social standing. Sara was intrigued as to what she might be talking about. Then it dawned on her—all those babies in the jars. Polly was working in a back-alley abortion clinic, and apparently her daughter was one of her patients. Polly wrote that Samantha, at seventeen, found herself pregnant. She refused to tell her mother the father's name, but Polly had a good idea. She had gotten up a few times in the middle of the nigh to find Henry coming out of Samantha's room. He was molesting her, or at least that was the conclusion Polly had come to. That was the reason for the fight the day she tried to kill him.

Sara read on, completely engulfed in the diary. When Polly was hiding out, trying to change her appearance, Samantha and Henry were off living together. Polly found them living in a cabin in the hills of California and was convinced they had fallen in love with each other. Polly convinced Henry to return to the pink house and get some of his belongings. That's when she murdered him. Polly told Samantha that he ran away without her and agreed to end the pregnancy. Samantha ended up dead next to her lover and father.

All this took place in Sara's house. The woman who owned the house agreed to leave the bodies where they were.

She knew Polly had a lot of stuff on her that could put her away for a long time. It didn't help that Polly threatened to kill her entire family as well. Both houses were tied together by love, greed, and murder.

Sara just sat there with this diary in her hand, stunned at what she'd read. She felt that Polly was somehow warning her from the grave to keep quiet. Sara felt the pit of her stomach sour and wanted to cry. The whole thing made her sick. How could a father rape his own daughter and then try to live with her as man and wife? The whole thing was appalling.

Sara closed the diary and set it aside. She was unsure of what to do. She decided to call Sergeant Allen in the morning, after she'd had time away from what she had just read.

Sara lay down on the couch and must have fallen asleep, for when she awoke, the diary was lying next to her. Except one thing was different: It was opened to the last few pages. Sara tried to read them, but the room was dark. She reached over and turned on the living room light. Then she headed for the bathroom, making a stop in her bedroom to don pajamas and a robe. She also needed food. It was 9 p.m. The whole day seemed like a blur to her.

Awakened Dreams

While in the bathroom freshening up, Sara heard a knock at her door. It was Bill. Ann was going to rehab in the morning, and she should be home in about two weeks if she does as well as they expected her to. Sara gave her dad a hug and let him know his laundry was done and on top of the dryer. Bill gave her the strangest look.

"Sara, my laundry has been done for three days. Don't you remember?"

"Oh, I just forgot, that's all."

After her dad left, Sara went into her office and looked at her calendar. She somehow lost three days. What the heck happened, and why couldn't she remember anything? She sat on the couch trying to remember something, anything of the last several days. Nothing came to mind. She just sat there dazed and feeling very alone.

The next day she woke up, got dressed, and went into the office early. She needed to speak with her boss, but he hadn't been in the office for two days. No one knew where he was, not even his wife who had filed a missing persons' report.

"Oh, my God, you're kidding me," Sara exclaimed. "Did he say he had a business meeting somewhere or something?" Everyone just stared at Sara.

"OK, what's going on here? Somebody better tell me, and tell me now."

"Sara, the last person Mr. Hall said he was going to see was you."

"What!" Sara cried. "I never saw him; he never came to my house."

"Well, the police would like to talk to you about the disappearance. We've been trying to call you for two days but you haven't answered your phone. And the police said they went to your house, but you didn't answer your door."

Sara was confused and frightened. "Maybe I was in the basement or something and I didn't hear the doorbell. Will somebody please call them so I can get all this taken care of?"

It just so happened it was Sergeant Allen who arrived and questioned Sara, the same sergeant that came to her home about the bodies that were discovered in her canning cellar. Sara assured him she hadn't seen her boss in at least four days. Sara told him she had been at home in bed with a severe cold, and was knocked out on cold medicine. That's why she didn't hear them knocking. She decided not to mention the diary at that point. The fact her boss was missing was enough.

The sergeant left and told her he would be in touch if he needed to ask her any more questions. Sara then made sure that whatever Mr. Hall was working on was completed and went home. She decided to call Sergeant Allen, and he stopped by to see the diary. He said he could now close the case; he had a motive and basically a written confession of the murders. He thanked her and was walking down the stairs to leave when he smelled something horrible. Sara was standing at the top of the stairs and smelled that same offensive odor. She said she thought she had a pipe backing up. He told her she should get that looked at right away. She assured him she would, and he left.

Sara decided to work at home the next day. She spoke with her secretary to find out if the boss had been located yet, but he was still missing. She was distant when Sara spoke with her, and Sara knew everyone was talking about her. Sara didn't care. She had other things to worry about. The stink from the backed-up water or sewer pipes was getting worse, almost unbearable. Amber couldn't take the smell any more and threatened to move if something wasn't done about it. Sara went to the hardware store and got some lye, which took care of the problem temporarily.

The bright spot in Sara's life was that her mom was doing well in rehab and was about to come home. She would have to walk with a cane for a while, but she got around beautifully. Sara was there to greet her the day she was due to come home, with flowers in hand. She helped Bill get Ann situated, cleaned up their apartment, and gathered laundry to take downstairs. She didn't want her parents to worry about anything for a while.

Sara placed her mom's laundry in the washer, and decided to check the newly constructed staircase that lead to the roof patio. She began climbing the stairs, thinking she wanted to do something really special with the patio, like an enclosed gazebo. She had seen one she liked that was fairly reasonably priced. Sara reached the roof, it was peaceful and quiet, a nice place to go and get away from it all. Sara sat down in one of the chairs and looked around, trying to decide where she might put the gazebo. When she found the perfect spot, she ran downstairs and went online to try and order one. She found exactly what she wanted, but the company didn't do installation. Sara then called Tom and asked him about hiring some men to put it up for her. He said it shouldn't be a problem. Sara tried to start a conversation with him, but he was short with her and told her he was in the middle of something; he would talk to her later. She felt a pit in the middle of her stomach. She wasn't used to Tom just blowing her off like that.

Sara tried to put the call out of her mind as she went back downstairs to finish her mom's laundry. After folding all the clothes and putting them into the basket, Sara proceeded to head back to her parents' apartment. She was stopped short by a voice that sounded like it was coming from a child, saying, "He's cheating on you, and now he's going to move far, far away, and you'll never see him again."

Sara quickly turned toward the voice, almost falling down the stairs. "Who's there? Is someone there?" she yelled. No answer. 'Okay, now I'm hearing things again. Great!' she said to herself. Sara turned to go back upstairs and again was almost knocked over, only this time it was by a woman. Or, rather, a ghostly, transparent figure standing at the top of the basement stairs. She seemed to be floating a foot off the ground.

She pointed her finger at Sara and said, "You're a fool. He's been cheating on you, and when he's with her, they laugh at you. They think you're funny." Then she disappeared as quickly as she appeared.

Sara slowly walked upstairs, dropped off the clothes with her mom, and told Ann she had to go to her apartment for a minute. Sara went upstairs and called Tom. A woman picked up the phone, and she was indeed laughing. Sara slammed down the phone and sat on the couch. She had never been so mad in her life, and thoughts of ways to make Tom pay began to run through her mind. She quickly put them in the back of her mind and went downstairs to see if her mom needed any help.

Sara managed to keep her deepest, sickest thoughts and ideas to herself; she didn't want to let them out until she was ready. She had plans for all the people she truly despised and some wonderful ideas on how to get rid of them. Entertaining these ideas really was her way of protecting herself when she was feeling hurt. And having a woman answer Tom's phone was pretty painful. She loved him and wanted to make a life with him. Now she really didn't know what to do.

The week came and went with no more ghosts or bad dreams. Amber came to visit and gave Sara several months' worth of rent. Sara invited Amber in for tea and told her about her plans for the gazebo. Amber was excited and wanted to have a housewarming party for Sara, which made Sara feel wonderful. The gazebo was set to be put up next week. Amber told her she would have the housewarming party possibly a week or two afterwards.

"I'll invite everyone in the building, plus some of my actor friends," Amber said. "It will be good for you to meet some new people."

When Amber left a couple hours later, she headed back to her apartment, gathered her laundry, and headed downstairs. She hated going into the basement by herself; it was creepy down there. As she got close to the basement door, she heard the dryer door slam shut. She opened the basement door and yelled, "Hey, who's down there?"

"Hi, Amber, it's only me."

"Me who?" she called.

"Tom."

Amber smiled and headed downstairs. "Hey, what's up, Tom?"

"Not much. What about you?"

Tom looked so handsome, Amber thought, as he leaned against the dryer. Tom was wearing a white T-shirt that showed every curve of his muscles and a form-fitting pair of jeans. Amber was very attracted to him. She dropped her laundry onto the ground, and it made an eerie echoing noise. They both stopped and looked around.

Amber looked at Tom and said, "I hate this basement."

"Yeah, it is a little eerie," Tom replied.

"And it smells terrible!"

"Sara was going to have a plumber come in and check things out, and I don't know if she ever did."

"Apparently not," Amber replied. "Tom, how would you like to have dinner with me tonight?"

"I think I would like that," Tom replied.

"Okay, how about seven? What kind of food do you like?"

"Anything is good. I'm not picky. Surprise me."

Unbeknownst to Tom and Amber, Sara was standing at the top of the stairs and everything they said. All she could thing about was what she heard earlier, that Tom was a cheater. Sara felt like a fool. She would make them pay for making her look like an idiot. She took a few deep breaths and headed down the basement stairs. Both Amber and Tom looked up, surprised to see her and feeling a bit guilty.

"Hey, Sara. What brings you down here?" Tom asked, noticing she wasn't carrying a laundry basket.

"I just came down to get one of the old books left down here. I felt like reading something, and I've read everything in my apartment."

Tom and Amber just sat on the couch in silence. The tension was so thick, you could almost cut it with a knife.

"Well, see you both later," Tom said when he couldn't take it azny more. "I've got some things to do."

"Bye, Tom." Amber said. Sara noticed a big smile on her face when she said that. She knew what was going on, and she was going to have to do something about it. When the time was right.

Amber sat on the couch and opened up a magazine. "Hey, Sara, it smells like something is backing up down here. Tom said you were going to get a plumber down here. Did you ever do that?"

"Not yet." Sara was in the corner looking through boxes of old dusty books, but staring directly at Amber with a look of pure evil on her face. Jealousy was taking over—and thoughts of murder. Sara was the only one who was going to be with Tom. Amber needed to leave him alone or be taken out of the picture somehow. But that was for another time.

Sara stood up with a copy of Edgar Allen Poe's collection in her hands. She loved his dark writings, and she felt in the mood for him. Sara told Amber she would see her later; Amber never even looked up from her magazine as she replied, "Yeah, see you, Sara."

A few days later, Sara received a surprise visit from Sergeant Allen. He needed to ask her more questions about her boss's disappearance.

"Sara, I'm confused about something," he began.

"What?" Sara asked.

"Mr. Hall told his secretary he was going to stop here on his way to the courthouse. Were you home that day?"

"Yes, I told you I was, but he never made it here."

"Well, I just spoke with your neighbor Amber, and she said she saw him going into your apartment. She apparently looked out her door when she heard someone coming up the front steps and saw him enter your apartment. Were you here, or did he make a habit of entering your apartment? Did he have a key?"

"No, he didn't have a key," she replied.

"Are you sure you weren't having an affair with him?" Sgt. Allen inquired.

"Absolutely not!" Sara cried. "I've never had an affair with my boss!"

"Okay, sorry. I have to ask, that's all," he replied. "I'm just trying to find him. Apparently he also took some money with him when he left—half a million dollars to be exact."

"Wow!" Sara exclaimed. "Sounds like he's off having fun somewhere. Was he having problems with his wife?"

"Not as far as she was concerned." Sgt. Allen answered. Soon thereafter he left, apparently satisfied with Sara's responses. Meanwhile, Sara felt uneasy about the whole encounter, like he was digging for something and wanted to pin it on her. Sara was glad to see him leave. She was getting tired of his questions, and she had bigger fish to fry.

Amber was trying to figure out what to wear for her date with Tom. She'd always had a secret crush on him and thought he was one of the best looking men she had ever seen. Amber just hoped he wasn't still in love with Sara and using her as a rebound person. She had lived that nightmare before and didn't want to be there again. She finally picked out a sexy black spaghetti strap dress. She was going to look hot tonight.

Tom was unsure of the date. He still loved Sara and thought of her on a daily basis. He just didn't want to be rude to Amber. He'd always thought she was a little self-centered, but he was going to try and make the best of it.
As he was getting dressed, he heard something kind of odd, like something heavy was being dragged down the stairs. But he dismissed it. It was six o'clock, and he still had an hour

before he had to meet Amber. He was making himself a cup of coffee when he heard a knock at the door. It was Sara.

"Hi," she said. "I think I got some of your mail by accident." She handed him some letters and magazines.

"Thanks. Do you want to come in?" Tom asked.

"No, I don't want to bother you. You look like you're on your way out."

Tom was looking at the ground, afraid to look at Sara.

"Yeah, I have a date," Tom said.

"Oh," Sara said in a low but sad voice. "Well, I hope you have a good time. You deserve it."

Tom looked up at Sara and opened his mouth to say something, but nothing came out. He just looked at her and said, "Thanks. See you later, okay?"

Sara looked him and replied halfheartedly, "Sure." She turned and headed back upstairs to her apartment. She could feel the blood beginning to rise and her face becoming flushed. Anger began to consume her and fill her with a need for revenge she never thought she could have. One way or the other, she thought, everyone was going to pay.

A MISSING PERSON

Seven came and went, but Amber was nowhere to be found. Tom headed upstairs to Amber's apartment and found a note taped to her door. It read: "Tom, had to go out of town on an emergency shoot. I'll call you when I get back, maybe we can reschedule our date. I'm really sorry—it couldn't be helped, Amber." Tom quickly snatched the letter off the door.

"Crap," he said aloud. "Why didn't she just come down and tell me this and not leave me hanging like this?" Well, that explains the something heavy being dragged down the stairs, he thought. It was Amber's luggage. Tom crumpled up the note, threw it on the ground, and stomped back to his apartment.

Sara, standing in her apartment with her ear pressed to the front door, heard everything Tom said. She had a smile on her face. Amber had stood Tom up. This was the best thing she had heard in a long time.

Tom felt like he was striking out all over the place. Even though he still cared about Sara, she wasn't the same sweet girl he first fell in love with, and he doubted things could work out with her. So he agreed to go out with Amber, only to be jilted at the last minute. Tom changed his clothes, went into the living room, and made himself a stiff drink.

In the days that followed, Tom was able to get his workers over to the apartment building to get Sara's gazebo up and mounted to the roof. After they constructed the gazebo, Sara sat up there for hours; she enjoyed the fresh breeze and the quiet. She could be in her own world, and she loved it.

Sara was sitting up on the patio one afternoon enjoying a glass of wine when she thought she heard someone coming. When she turned to see who it was, there was nobody there. Sara stood up, walked over to the door, and called to see if anyone was walking down the stairs, but nobody answered. "I must be hearing things," she thought as she returned to her chair and her glass of wine. When she looked over, she realized someone was sitting in the chair next to her. It was Polly, except she was almost transparent. Polly looked at Sara and said, "You've got to finish what you started. Don't let anyone stop you now, not your parents or Tom or Sgt. Allen. Finish what you started," and she disappeared. Sara raised her glass of wine toward where Polly was sitting and said, "Don't worry, I will."

SARA'S PARENTS' NIGHTMARE

Two weeks passed, and no one had heard from either Amber or Sara's boss. Sara just went about her business without seeming concerned, which worried her parents. One day, Ann waited for Sara to come home from work. She needed to talk to her. Sara came home at around five with her arms full of groceries. As she began climbing the stairs, Ann popped her head out of her apartment.

"Sara, can I talk to you?"

"Sure, Mom, give me a minute to put this stuff away and I'll come down."

Ann detected a note of irritation in Sara's voice and asked, "Honey, are you okay? You sound mad about something."

"No, Mom, I'm not mad!" Sara exclaimed in a voice that certainly sounded angry.

An hour later, Sara finally went down to see what Ann wanted. From the looks on her parents' faces, she felt like she was walking into the lions' den, awaiting attack.

"Honey, come sit down. We need to talk," Bill said. Sara sat down with a wary look on her face; she didn't know what her parents were up to.

"Listen, honey," Ann said. "We're worried about you. Lately you seem distant and not yourself."

"Mom, I'm fine," Sara replied, exasperated. "What makes you think anything is wrong?"

"Well, for one thing, you lied to the police about your boss coming over, and that's not at all like you."

"Mom, my boss never came to my apartment. I wasn't lying!"

"Sara, I let him in the front door myself. He headed upstairs, and I heard you let him in."

"Mom, you're the one who's lying, and you know that." Sara stood up and walked into the kitchen. She was so upset with the both of them, she could feel the blood rising up and her face turning red with anger.

Bill called after her, "Honey, we just want to know what's going on with you, that's all. We want to help if we can."

"Mom, Dad, I'm fine. Really you don't have to worry about me." Sara walked back into the living room. She had a blank look on her face, and a butcher knife in her hand. Her parents never saw it coming. Sara raised the knife and buried it into the back of her dad. Her mom turned and tried to scream, and Sara drove the knife down her mom's throat. Both were killed instantly. "Now I don't have to worry about them anymore," she said aloud. She turned to see Polly standing there.

Polly turned to her and said, "You must finish what you started."

Sara slowly walked over to the sink and washed the blood from her hands and the knife. Then she took the vinyl tablecloth from the dining room table and laid it gently on the ground. Sara would have to wait until Tom was in bed to move the bodies. Sara went back to her parents' apartment, made a pot of coffee, and sat down in the living room chair. She just stared at her parents.

"Why did you make me do this to you?" she asked their dead, bleeding corpses. "I finally give you a normal life, but you can't stay out of mine."

Sara went over and slapped her mom across the face. Blood went everywhere. "See what you made me do?" she screamed. "After all those times I hid in the closet waiting for your crazy ass to come out of whatever psychotic episode you were having, you turn on me. Well, I guess I showed you who's boss, didn't I?"

Sara took her by the hair, dragged her over to the tablecloth, and wrapped Ann up like she was a carpet. Sara looked up at Polly and said, "I'm finishing the job."

Polly replied, "You are not done," and disappeared. Sara knew what she was talking about. She had one more thing to do. Sara moved the bodies to a location she thought would be nice for them; after all, they were still her parents. Then she went back to her parents' apartment and cleaned up the blood as best she could. What she couldn't get out, she covered up. Sara looked at her watch; it was two in the morning. She was tired and decided to go to bed. She would make up some excuse to Tom in the morning why Bill wasn't going to be at work.

Polly appeared in her bedroom and said, "You're not done yet."

Sara turned over and fell asleep; she woke up at six in the morning, phoned Tom, and told him Ann and Bill had to leave town. An emergency came up, and they went back to Chicago for a week or so to check on one of Bill's old work buddies who was sick. Sara told him he did apologize and didn't mean to leave Tom in a mess with one man down. Tom told Sara not to worry about it; he was always understanding about those kinds of things.

A week passed, and Sara got a call from Tom asking if she had heard from Bill. She said they were scheduled to come back tomorrow. He then asked her if she had heard from Amber.

"She went out on another movie shoot, didn't she? I know she left me several months of rent. She wouldn't have done that unless she was going to be gone for a while."

"Well, I just thought I would ask, that's all." Tom paused a second, then asked, "Sara, did you ever have a plumber come and look at the pipes downstairs? I noticed a pretty bad smell downstairs. It smells like the problem is getting worse."

"They will be here next week; hopefully they'll be able to take care of the problem."

"Okay, well, see you later then, Sara; take care of yourself."

"Thanks. You, too, Tom."

Sara was trying to take care of all the things she needed to, like Polly said she should. Her parents were gone. Ben had run away or was hiding out somewhere; she hadn't seen him in days. Sara decided she needed some quiet time to think about everything, so she headed to the rooftop patio with a bottle of wine and a glass.

As she expected, Polly joined her. "You've taken care of a few of the problems, but you still have one more to go," she said, then disappeared as fast as she appeared. Sara was getting tired of Polly. She was going to have to do something about her as well.

TOM GETS TOO CLOSE

Another week passed, and Tom called and left messages for Sara every day. Sara didn't bother even calling him back. When he stopped by or they ran into each other, she just kept telling him her parents were still in Chicago and not to worry because they would be home soon. Tom could no longer accept her explanation. He knew, deep down, something was wrong, and he was going to find out the truth.

One day, when Sara headed down the basement to do some laundry, she noticed the odor was not nearly as potent.

One less thing for Tom to complain about, she thought. Sara was sitting on the couch, waiting for her laundry to be done, when Polly appeared.

"Polly," Sara asked, "what really happened down here, and what was going on with your daughter and your husband?" She wanted to hear it straight from the source.

Polly didn't respond; she just kept staring at Sara with black eyes and a transparent body. She never said a word about what really happened, but Sara knew from reading the old newspaper articles. And Polly knew she knew.

On her way back upstairs later, Sara saw Tom trying to jimmy his way into her parents' apartment.

"Tom, what the hell are you doing?" she asked him.

"Listen, I think something is terribly wrong. Your dad wouldn't have just up and left like that. He's very responsible about his job, not to mention he really loves his work."

Sara looked at Tom and said, "Okay, I didn't want to say anything, but my mom is sick again. She's back in the hospital, only they are in Chicago. They are stuck there because my mom got sick while they were there. As soon as she gets better, they'll come home. Tom, I hope you understand. Please don't fire my dad. He loves working for you, but when this happens he sometimes forgets his other obligations and focuses fully on my mom."

"Sara, I understand. I just want to talk to him and make sure he doesn't need anything, that's all."

"They're okay," Sara said. "I'll make sure they don't need anything. Don't worry, I'm taking care of them."

Sara had a funny look on her face when she said these last words, which made Tom really concerned. Something not had happened to Ann and Bill, and at the hands of their own daughter, and he was determined to find out what it was.

Tom waited until Sara was in her apartment, in bed, and then headed down to the basement. He took the flashlight off the ledge on his way down and began looking around but didn't find much. Then he decided to check out Bill and Ann's apartment. Bill gave Tom a key the day he fell in the bathroom, for emergency reasons. When he entered the apartment and turned on the light, he immediately noticed a strong smell of bleach. He saw that the carpets were stained with a brown substance, as was the couch. Something was cleaned up here, he thought. What was it? Could it be blood? Tom shuddered at the thought.

Next, Tom headed toward the new staircase his company had built. He walked up the staircase only to find a padlock on the door that led to the rooftop patio. How odd, he thought. What was up there that the world could not see? What was Sara trying to hide? Tom was determined to find out.

A few days later, Sara decided to go and have a glass of wine on the rooftop. She needed to clear her head. Tom had become very curious about Sara's activities, stopping by for no reason, asking her how she was doing. Little did she know he had booked a flight for Chicago in search of Bill and Ann. But before he left, he wanted to check out the rooftop patio. Tom knew Sara was hiding something; he just didn't know what. But he was going to find out. If he found what he was looking for up on that patio, he might not have to take a trip to Chicago. At least that's what he thought.

When he was sure Sara was asleep, he took some bolt cutters up the stairs that lead to the rooftop patio and cut away the large lock, making a large clink as the lock hit the ground. After waiting a few minutes to make sure he hadn't awakened Sara, Tom slowly opened the door and walked onto the roof. He was uncertain what Sara was hiding there, but he was going to find out tonight. Tom flipped on a switch that lit up the patio. It was quite beautiful, but he saw something odd—figures sitting around a table inside the gazebo.

When Tom went to see who it was, the smell almost made him vomit. But the scene was even more horrid. There, sitting in a perfect circle, were Amber, Bill, Ann, and some other man Tom didn't recognize. Could it be Sara's boss? Tom remembered being questioned about his disappearance. They had been dead for a while; all of them were covered in flies and maggots. The unidentified man's throat had been cut.

Tom ran to the edge of the roof and vomited. Sara was responsible for all this carnage, and he had to call the police. Tom was heading back to the door that lead downstairs when it slammed shut. Tom tried to open it, but it was locked from the inside. Sara must have found out he was there.

He began to look around for anything he might use to break the door down with. Around the side of the door, he found an axe. A worker must have lrft it there. Tom took the axe and began to break the door down. It took him forever, like someone was holding it shut, but he finally succeeded. Tom decided he needed to speak with Sara before he called the police, just to make sure the woman he once loved was guilty. Tom knocked on Sara's door. No answer.

Sara jumped out of bed, awakened by someone trying to break into her apartment. She could hear the frame of the door being torn apart and began to panic. Then she heard footsteps and knew the intruder was getting closer to her. In the dim light, she saw someone step into her bedroom entrance. She couldn't make out the face, but she could see the person was big and was carrying something. Finally the person took another step and the bathroom light revealed his identity. It was Tom, and he had an axe resting on his shoulder.

Sara began to scream at him. "What are you doing here? Why did you break into my apartment? You scared me half to death!" Tom only looked at her with a blank stare, black eyes, and a grin on his face that scared her to death. Sara tried to scramble out of bed but got caught in the covers and fell head first out of bed, striking her head on her bedside table. Sara fought with all her might not to pass out and had never been so terrified in her life.

Tom looked at her and said, "Maybe this is how your victims felt right before you killed them."

Sara looked at Tom but didn't hear one word he said. Was this a dream, or was she awake? She didn't know anymore. Did Polly put Tom up to this like she had done to her so many times? Polly had made Sara do many things, or was that all just a dream, too?

Sara looked at Tom and knew he was going to kill her. Not just hurt her, but kill her. As if Tom read he mind, he said, "I would rather you be dead than in prison or a mental hospital for the rest of your life. I love you too much to see you go through that."

Sara again couldn't hear one word Tom said. She just knew she had to protect herself one way or another. After Tom relentlessly chased her around her apartment, she was able to get her gun from the closet. She fired one shot into Tom's head, and he dropped like a rag doll. Sara still had the gun in her hand when the police arrived. She didn't drop it fast enough and ended up getting shot in the hand.

Sara passed out from the pain. When she woke up, the one thing she was sure of was the pain. Excruciating pain in her right thigh and right hand. Sara tried to roll over but couldn't. Her left hand was attached to something. She turned her head and could see a figure sitting next to her.

"Hey, where am I? What happened?"

Whoever was next to her got up and walked out of the room. Five minutes later, a well-dressed man walked in. Sara looked straight at him but still couldn't seem to focus and see his face.

"Sara Miles?"

She said, "Yes."

"I'm Detective Steven Godfrey." The detective proceeded to read Sara her Miranda rights and place her under arrest for five counts of murder in the first degree. Sara tried to free her left hand and realized she was cuffed to the bed railing.

Sara stared at the detective in horror; she couldn't believe this was happening to her. She didn't do anything wrong. Everyone tried to hurt her, and she was just trying to protect herself. When she was questioned about the murders, she said she didn't remember anything. She swore Polly was the one who told her to do everything.

It was a well known fact that Polly Mills wandered the neighborhood, haunting the area, but the neighbors said they hadn't had an encounter with her in years. They thought she had gone. They also said they sometimes saw her white cat, Ben, stalking the neighborhood.

Sara was found many times sitting in her room, stroking an imaginary cat and talking to it. She was also noticed talking to someone as she walked down the halls of the hospital. No one could ever figure out who it was, and she didn't elaborate. She just looked at them with a blank stare and black eyes and that smile, lost in herself and her own world, a world filled with women who wanted to save other women, and white cats with big blue eyes. Sara was in a happy place, not remembering the horror of her actions. It was better that way.

ABOUT THE AUTHOR

Annette Johnson lives in Wheatfield, Indiana, with her three grown children and husband. She is an animal lover and writer; she loves everything horror and thriller. For the past 10 years, she has also worked as an ER and ICU nurse. She feels there is no better joy than picking up a good book and not being able to put it down. Her hope is that she accomplished this.